# DARING DANIELLA

THE UNSETTLING OF GOLDEN RIVER - BOOK TWO

PIPPA GREATHOUSE

RUBY CAINE

Published by Blushing Books
An Imprint of
ABCD Graphics and Design, Inc.
A Virginia Corporation
977 Seminole Trail #233
Charlottesville, VA 22901

©2019 by ABCD Graphics and Design, Inc.
Pippa Greathouse and Ruby Caine
All rights reserved.

No part of the book may be reproduced or transmitted in any form or by any means, electronic or mechanical, including photocopying, recording, or by any information storage and retrieval system, without permission in writing from the publisher. The trademark Blushing Books is pending in the US Patent and Trademark Office.

Pippa Greathouse
Ruby Caine
Daring Daniella

EBook ISBN: 978-1-61258-983-1
Print ISBN: 978-1-64563-037-1
v1

Cover Art by ABCD Graphics & Design
This book contains fantasy themes appropriate for mature readers only. Nothing in this book should be interpreted as Blushing Books' or the author's advocating any non-consensual sexual activity.

# PROLOGUE

DISILLUSIONED...

Daniella stood at the window, looking toward the path that led to the small town of Golden River. Her mind was occupied with disquiet as she fingered the material that lined her curtains. They could certainly use a new lining. Another look outside brought a downturn to her lips.

The brides were here now. There were ten of them, and they were working hard to turn the heads of every available man in town. The competition among them was fierce as they played at being coy and teased. Was Caleb impressed by them, too? Daniella's frown increased. He certainly seemed to be paying less attention to her now.

She shook her head and turned back to the mirror, staring at her reflection. She had always thought her hair a mousy brown, with eyes that matched, even if people said they twinkled when she smiled. Her brothers had confirmed it by calling her 'mouse' when they wanted to irritate her. A sigh escaped, just as she heard a knock on the door.

"Come in."

Jeddah's beautiful golden head popped around the doorway, frowning. "You look sad, Danny. What is it?"

Daniella plopped down on the bed on her belly, her small ankles waving in the air. "Just having pity for myself, that's all. I was thinking of all the beautiful brides in town. Caleb hasn't even spoken to me in the past two days. I'll bet he's smitten with some of them. And the rest of the men in town don't come out here much, either." She turned to face her friend. "Jeddah, you and I were the first two brides to come here. And neither of us have a proposal yet."

Jeddah's mouth turned up at the corners. "I have my heart set on Noah. I know. I know I said I would marry the richest man in town." A musical laugh filled the room. "In truth, there don't seem to be any."

Danny nodded. "I told you, didn't I? They're all poor. But I've been thinking, Jeddah. What's money if you have a man who is rich but cares nothing about you? Look at Mayor Blackaby. He might have a little, but he wouldn't spend it on a wife if his life depended on it. He doesn't even ride his mule anymore; he bought a donkey because he got a cheaper price, and he's tried to sell the mule, but no one will pay his price for it. So, he rides the donkey everywhere, even though he's too big for it and it only moves when it wants to. He's the only one in town who has a suit to his name—well, I guess that isn't true, exactly. Tobias has one, but I've never seen him wear it except to marry Obie."

"The mayor is a louse, Danny, and you know it. Some of the new girls are even trying to get his attention. I won't. I want Noah. Yes, I do wish he was a little...richer, but I've set my sights on him. So, there it is." Her expression changed, and she appeared thoughtful. "I do know what you mean about the other girls, however. One of them..." She silenced abruptly and bit down on her lip.

Daniella frowned. "If you're going to say one of them has her eye on either Caleb or Noah, I'll find her—"

"No, no—that's not what I was going to say. The truth is I was going to make a confession." Sitting down on the bed, she glanced up at her friend with a pout. "I sort of—sent a letter home, hoping my mother would read it to some of her friends and let word get around."

Daniella's eyes widened. "What did you tell them?"

"Um, I sort of said that I was going to marry Noah, and that he was…well off, and a man who commanded power and respect, and—"

"That much is true, Jeddah. Everyone respects him and loves him."

"It's just that one of the new brides who arrived is from my home town. And I wrote that letter right after we came here. And I think she knows about it because she looks at me slyly every time I see her."

"Oh, Jeddah. That's not good."

They sat in silence a moment, and Danny reached over to pat her hand.

"Well, I've set mine on Caleb, too, but it doesn't seem to be doing me any good, for all my efforts." She let a giggle escape. "Look at us. The first two brides in Golden River in who knows how long, and there have been two marriages since we've been here. And neither of them included us. I'm half afraid Caleb will choose one of the new girls. They're ever so much lovelier than I."

Jeddah sat up straight. "Danny, you're feeling sorry for yourself, and I won't have it." Grabbing Daniella's wrist, she pulled her back up to her feet and dragged her to the mirror. "Look."

Daniella groaned. "I have been. That's why I'm in such a poor state of mind." Her eyes began to sparkle with tears, and she turned away. "And because Caleb is ignoring me."

Jeddah's shoulders sagged as she shook her head from side to side. "Caleb loves you, Danny. It's obvious to anyone who sits at the dinner table every single night and sees how he watches you. Every time one of the other men speaks to you, he becomes green with jealousy. He sees you as his."

Danny turned, her face hopeful. "Do you really think so?" she whispered.

Jeddah smiled. "Oh, Danny. I don't think. I know."

# CHAPTER 1

PRESSURED...

Caleb Matthews scowled as he slammed the cell door shut on his prisoner. "I figure I'm a reasonable man. Wouldn't you agree?" He pulled off his Stetson and brushed his sandy hair out of his eyes. Exhaling with frustration, he looked lost in thought.

The bearded man behind bars regarded him soberly. "Can't say for sure, since we only just met and all. If I was to make a guess, I'd say you were fairly reasonable, seeing as you didn't rough me up any once you figured me for a wanted man. But I have to tell you, the way you bowed up at my question about you getting hitched did scare me a might, at first."

Caleb's face reddened as he glared at the prisoner he'd just locked up. "All I asked for was a yes or no. So, you can keep your opinions to yourself." He walked back to the front of the office.

"Is that the man who is wanted for robbing the bank in Sacramento?" Sheriff Tobias Madison began flipping through the wanted posters. He whistled when he located one with the description of the man his deputy and good friend had just brought in. "Where did you find him?"

"He was hiding out behind the new hotel, watching the gaggle of geese—excuse me—brides, nesting there." Caleb grabbed a chair from behind the desk and turned it so he was straddling it, his elbows crossed over the back. "Well, Sheriff, I'm waiting for an answer."

Tobias glanced up from the poster detailing the robbery. "Remind me what the question was again. My mind is mush these days, my friend. Obedience is sick as a dog, and it has me befuddled."

"Is she still retching all the time?" With all the hoopla going on in his own life, Caleb had forgotten the sheriff's new bride was expecting. He felt guilty for not being more supportive of his friend's plight.

Tobias nodded. "Noah stopped by to check on her this morning. Obie was so thrilled by the gesture, she rushed to fix him a cup of coffee. I have warned her to avoid the kitchen because the slightest odor upsets her stomach. The smell of black coffee did her in. The preacher left wearing both the coffee and a good deal of the milk and biscuits my wife had for breakfast. The woman is so dang tiny. Where does she store all this stuff that comes back up?"

Caleb tried not to laugh, but it was satisfying to know other men were suffering the effects of dealing with the original Golden River brides. About six months before, the mayor had come up with a doltish scheme to ensure the town grew and prospered, even though the gold mines which brought most of the settlers here had dried up. The politician collected a tidy sum from suckers like himself, Caleb remembered. But he wasn't the only one to support it. The money was supposed to be used to send off for brides to come here—and likely, some of it was, but not all. Putting that thought aside, however, Caleb returned to thinking about the arrival of the first brides. Nothing had been the same since.

Daniella Abcott had arrived, soon afterward, and had promptly stolen his clothes and his sanity. Jeddah Cromwell and Danny, as most people called her, had answered the mayor's advertisement. They'd ended up staying with Obedience Bartlett, who had come west to help her aunt run one of two ranches outside town. The three women had no sooner settled in at the ranch of Faith Bartlett than mischief ensued.

Obie had managed to bury a perfectly good wedge deep into a stump while trying to chop wood. There wasn't a man in all of Golden River who could get it free, and nearly all had tried at one time or another. Then Daniella had decided to mend fences with barbed wire, resulting in Obie getting her arm sliced open. Next, Daniella had pulled Jeddah into another scheme and stolen the clothes of both himself and Noah, while they were swimming in the river—all within the first forty-eight hours of the ladies' arrival. Caleb sighed.

It was only the beginning.

"Poor Noah." Caleb chuckled, finding his first genuine smile in weeks. "He still only has one shirt and one set of trousers to his name. But if Daniella and Jeddah hadn't stolen our clothes and destroyed them so they could make themselves breeches, Noah could look better when he preaches on Sunday morning. It would serve those young ladies right if we tanned their hides all over again. When I recall catching them strutting around in those obscene clothes, showing off their feminine curves on the very night they were kidnapped by rustlers—"

"Take a deep breath, Caleb. You are much too tense these days. You used to be so reasonable, but lately, you seem to explode like dynamite where the brides are concerned." The sheriff opened his top desk drawer and pulled out two glasses and a bottle of whiskey. Pouring them each a shot, he nudged one glass toward the deputy.

"Any man in my position *would* lose all reason. Do you know what kind of week I've had? My life has been in shambles ever since you up and got married." Caleb downed his measure of liquor in one gulp before helping himself to more.

Tobias cocked his head to one side and cleared his throat. "Pardon, but how is my marrying Obedience ruining *your* life?" He swirled the liquid in his glass and smiled. "Made *my* life much nicer," he added, drinking down the contents of his own glass. "Please tell me Obie hasn't thrown up all over you again."

"No, she hasn't. Not lately. It's you and Sterling who mucked things up. When the mayor sent off for the brides, you fought the notion every step of the way. You swore you'd send them back home. But you took one look at Obedience Bartlett and fell in line like a whipped mule. You up and married her before either of the official brides had a chance to settle in. Then Sterling married Faith. How does it feel to have a wife who tells you what to do?"

Tobias stared. "Does she? I wasn't aware of that."

Caleb rolled his eyes. "And now everyone in town expects me to rush down the altar, myself, to marry Daniella."

"You were one of the men who put in money to send for the brides," Tobias said fiercely. "I take offence at you comparing me to a whipped mule. Danny picked you as her future husband, another part of the stupid scheme you and the rest of the men let the mayor stipulate."

Caleb studied his glass and turned to glare at Tobias. "I'm not a stallion or bull to be paraded about so some slip of a girl can pick me out as her prize. When and if I marry, it will be on my terms. I am sick of repeating that fact time and again."

"You love Danny," the sheriff pointed out. "She loves you. Some would say you decided the 'when and the if' when you put money in the pot to send for the brides."

Caleb slammed the glass down on the wooden desk, causing the wanted posters to flutter off the edge. "Some would say? How about *all* would say?"

He tried to grab the bottle of whiskey to refill his glass, but the sheriff insisted on pouring it, giving him only a small portion. A few choice words escaped before beginning to list the times he had been cornered with questions about his impending marriage. "Old Howard got into a fight with Grayson, yesterday. It took me a good ten minutes to separate the two of them. Howard might be close to fifty, but he is as strong as a bull. I gave them both my standard lecture about public fighting. If they wanted to beat each other to death, they needed to leave the town's limits to do it. Finally, I asked if either of them had anything to say about their actions. Care to hear what each said?"

The sheriff had a keen mind. He gave his friend more whiskey. "Go ahead and let it out, buddy."

"When are you getting hitched? Maybe that'll keep you off our backs," Caleb scowled, mimicking old Howard's scruffy voice.

But his tale had just started. Soon, more details emerged, his frustration growing. "Last week, Fred, the skinny hermit who lives near the river, lost control of his wagon. It rolled over in a ditch, and he couldn't get it out. I stopped to give him a hand. The man has not spoken a word to me in the five years I have lived in this town, but he was full of questions that day. 'When you marryin' that girl, deputy?'" Now, Caleb's voice sounded deep and cocky.

The sheriff covered his mouth with his hand and turned away, but Caleb had already seen his grin. "It's not funny, Tobias. The brides weren't here more than a few hours before they caught wind of the plot afoot to snare me."

"Plot? You sound like you think the entire town is out to trap you, Deputy. I think you've had enough to drink today." The sheriff returned the bottle to the drawer and locked it shut, depositing the key into his pocket.

"Not the entire town." Caleb stood up and started pacing. "Just one brown-eyed, dark haired brat. She's plotting my demise, Tobias. I'm surprised she doesn't have my scalp hanging from her bedpost, already." He stopped for a moment, staring before remembering another confrontation.

"And listen to this! The pretty little chaperone watching over the brides pulled me aside the day of their arrival. She demanded I stop tempting her girls. It was hard, but I asked her nicely, *politely* even, to explain what the hell she meant. She didn't hold back." Now the deputy's voice grew shrill and high pitched. "The brides get to pick their husbands, and it's best for them to focus on available men. Since you are taken, you are only confusing them. And by the by, when are you getting married?"

Different encounters poured from him like a river reaching flood levels. The deputy continued. "I go to check on Faith. 'Married life *is* blissful, deputy. When are you going to stop stalling and marry Daniella?'" He glared toward the back room where the prisoner stood, eyeing him warily, and continued.

"Then the mayor sees me crossing the road. 'Hurry up, Matthews. When are you planning to tie the knot?' And even my buddy Noah. He sees me after Sunday service. Does he say, 'Good to see you here, buddy? Nice day today, buddy?' No. He says, 'Let me know when you and Daniella are ready to get married.'"

"This morning, on the way into town, I passed the telegraph office. He stopped me and handed me this." Caleb reached into his pocket and pulled out the paper. "Believe it or not, I got a telegram from my mother. She hates spending money, Tobias, since we were destitute for so many years. Yet she paid dearly to send me a personal inquiry. 'Hello, son. *Stop.* Been thinking of you. *Stop.* When are you going to give up and finally get married? *Stop.*' I want *grandchildren.*" He slammed the paper down on the desk in front of the sheriff, shouting, "*Stop!*"

Tobias was leaning back in his seat, shaking his head. "You've got it bad, Caleb. Relax."

"I'm trying. But you asked about the man I just shoved into the jail cell. Today, I was forced to realize just how out of control this entire situation has become. I was walking around town, minding my own business and not daring to get too close to the brides or their mother hen, when I saw a strange man lurking around the back of the hotel."

"Him?" Tobias jerked a thumb in the prisoner's direction.

"*Him.* Then I remembered the wanted posters which came in day before last. I recalled one of them was for a man who robbed a bank over in Sacramento. Hard to comprehend why anyone would choose to hide out here, in a town with no money in it, but he fit the description. So, I sneaked up on him and took him into custody."

Tobias glanced toward the jail cell and then back at Caleb. "And?"

"He confessed to everything, robbing the bank, hiding the money just outside of town, and trying to bide his time here until things blew over in Sacramento. He figured he could stay in Golden River without a lick of trouble because everyone knew the sheriff just got married and wasn't around and about as much. Then he looked me right in the eye and asked, 'Aren't you the deputy? I heard you were getting married next, so I figured it would be safe to hide out here.'"

A wide grin spread across Tobias' mouth. "Not easy being thought of as a whipped mule, eh?"

Caleb stopped pacing. "I'm not whipped yet." He shoved his hat back on his head and decided to put an end to the whole mess. "It's about time I pay little Miss Daniella a visit and lay down the law. I won't be rushed. If she loves me, waiting until the time is right should not be a problem."

Caleb turned toward the door to go outside, stopping at the sheriff's voice.

"And if it *is* a problem? Suppose she's tired of waiting and another man wants to snap her up?"

Caleb's mouth was a flat line. "She won't do that."

"You willing to take that chance?" Tobias' brow rose.

"She'll have to learn to deal with it," Caleb said, feeling a bit like a cad at his cold statement. He hated feeling caged in. Always had, probably always would.

Caleb stood, leaning against the doorway. The whiskey was taking its effect on his nerves, finally, and a mellow feeling replaced the anger he'd felt a few moments before. He barely noticed Tobias staring at him, his head cocked to one side.

He remembered the day the mayor had called a town hall meeting and talked about Golden River dying out. Miners were pulling out, and something had to be done soon, or the town would cease to be.

This town, poor but proud, had been the first place where Caleb had ever felt in control of his own destiny. The thought of it disappearing off the map had startled him. He got caught up in dreams of having a warm woman next to him on cold nights. He hadn't been with a woman in over a year. Before that, if he wanted to bed down with one, he had to make the long journey to Sacramento. It would be a damn sight more convenient to have someone closer to home. Not just a woman. A wife...

So, he'd added his funds to the pot to send off for brides, right before the sheriff showed up. Tobias hadn't hesitated to remind him about all the trouble associated with women. Golden River was still wild in so many ways. "Women from the east would likely die, like my first wife, Jenny," Tobias had said, "or flee after a few months of the harsh reality of living here."

Caleb was frowning as he thought of how it had crossed his mind; some of the other men *could* step up and marry the brides who came here. Then the town would have a better chance of surviving and he wouldn't have to deal with any of the troublesome issues a wife would bring. But did he really want that?

*It was a solid, logical plan.* And it would have worked, if he hadn't looked backward over his shoulder one day while bathing in the river and spotted an impish, dark-haired little brat gawking at him. Her beautiful brown eyes had locked on his backside, and damn, if she didn't seem to enjoy what she saw.

It was a good thing he was in the cold water at the time. His body had reacted immediately to Daniella's arrival. He'd had to stay in the water a bit longer than he wanted just to make sure he didn't embarrass himself when he exited. He'd intended to dress quickly and track her down. He wasn't sure if he wanted to give her a long, deep kiss or a sound spanking, but he was determined to find her.

Doing so was hampered. She had stolen the clothes hanging from the tree not far from the water's edge—clothes belonging to both himself and Noah—outsmarting them and allowing herself precious time to escape his wrath. When he'd finally tracked her down at Faith's ranch, one look told him he was in deep trouble. She'd looked him right in the eyes and lied, claiming she didn't have his things. Yet his heart still skipped a beat as he remembered the gentle sway of her full hips as she'd walked away.

Danny was just about perfect. She had a sharp wit, a zest for life, and no idea just how beautiful she truly was. He'd almost lost her when she was kidnapped by outlaws, but she didn't sit around waiting for him or the sheriff to come rescue her. Her bravery and intelligence helped save her life and the lives of Jeddah and Obedience, too.

Oh, hell," he cursed silently. He loved her. He adored her. "Now, what?"

"Now, you marry her." The sheriff's voice was full of mirth. "Of course, that's not *my* advice. *I'd* never say that. Not me." When Caleb turned to him with a withering glance, he chuckled. "My wife *told* me to."

Caleb rolled his eyes once more. "That's exactly what I mean."

"Ah," Tobias commented, staring out the window just as he had a moment earlier. "And take a look. The object of your affection isn't far away." A sly grin made its way across his face.

Caleb followed Tobias' gaze, seeing his beloved moving toward the mercantile across the street. Her beautiful chestnut hair peeked out from under a fancy bonnet. Even with her back to him, he could still picture the adorable dimple which appeared when she smiled. As she moved inside, a small gloved hand rose to wave at the shopkeeper. She began to move about the store, touching things just out of sight. Caleb's heart began beating faster.

What he did *not* see, because his gaze was so focused on Daniella, was the group of young ladies heading in his direction until one of them almost knocked him over. The group started giggling as he offered his apologies. They disappeared into the store, and he wondered if he should wait outside for Daniella. He didn't wish to tangle with the brides' chaperone again.

Several of them found their way toward his beautiful brat, and they admired something in her hands. Not that he cared all that much, he told himself, but Caleb tried to get a glimpse of what she held. Maybe he could come back later and purchase whatever she was admiring. His mother was always thrilled when his dad brought her little gifts.

Then, however, Daniella lifted it in the air to hold it up against the light of the window, and clear as day, he saw it. It was material, white cloth to be exact, the kind a woman might choose if she was making a special outfit like a wedding dress. He could almost hear her sweet, little voice asking, "When are you going to marry me?"

Any chance of being reasonable disappeared immediately. The deputy stormed into the building, grabbed the bolt of cloth out of her hand and slammed it back on the table she had pulled it from. "Now, listen here, you little brat." His hands were planted on his hips. The other women started gathering around to watch the excitement.

"Caleb! What's gotten into you? I was planning on purchasing that fabric to make—" Danny's cheeks tinged with scarlet as she spoke, seeing an audience gathering. Perhaps she didn't want any of the brides hearing them having a spat.

"You can forget it. Your little sewing project will wait until I am good and ready to ask." He yanked off his hat when he noticed the young ladies watching him. His voice lowered, but the brides compensated by taking a collective step forward. "Miss Daniella, I think it would be best for you to head back to the ranch this minute. I will come calling soon. You and I need to have a very important discussion."

One the brides sighed loudly. "How romantic, Deputy! You're about to propose. Though I think it quite rude of you to settle on whom you want to marry before you get to know the rest of us. You are in most of our top ten lists, you know. Of potential mates, that is."

Danny took a threatening step toward the girl who had just spoken. "Well, you can all just scratch him off, because he's already taken."

Caleb picked his little brat up in his arms and moved to the door, setting her down a few feet away from the group of brides. He scowled at her. "I never thought I would have to give this warning to women, but public brawling is not acceptable in Golden River."

But none of the girls seemed to be listening. "Is it true?" one demanded. "*Are* you taken?"

"Taken but not branded yet," he announced firmly. "Let's step outside, ladies. I think everyone in this town should hear what I'm about to say."

Another bride whispered, "Maybe he will announce when they're going to get married."

Caleb's back stiffened, and Daniella began stroking his arm in an effort to soothe him. She smiled up at him, and he was sure she was trying to sway him with her charms.

*It won't work*, he promised himself. *Not this time*. Caleb pulled her outside and called out to those citizens standing nearby, "I have an announcement to make. You can all stop asking when Miss Abcott and I are going to marry. It's our decision. When we are prepared to make a commitment, we'll let you know. Until then, the rest of you can kindly mind your own business."

He braced himself before looking down, fearing the hurt he would find on Daniella's face, but swore to himself he would not back down. The brides already looked mutinous. If they were pirates, he would be fed to the sharks before sundown.

His eyes fell to Daniella's face. What the others thought didn't matter to him. Only Danny did. He met her brown eyes and was speechless for a moment. She was nodding her agreement about his statement. Was she calling his bluff? Testing his resolve? Not understanding his determination? He leaned his forehead down to touch hers and spoke in a low voice so no one else could hear. "Daniella? Do you understand my meaning?"

She nodded, and he put an arm around her shoulders but didn't let her go. His voice in her ear was meant only for her. "Our marriage plans will be only between us and no one else. Hear me?" When she nodded eagerly, he gave her a quick kiss on the mouth. His voice rose again. "You, young lady, can put off your sewing plans until I give you my permission. I won't be manipulated. If you truly want to have me for a husband, you will wait until I ask you properly."

With that, he put his hat back on, gave her a quick kiss on the forehead this time, and jumped on Socks, his horse. The entire town was frowning at him as if he had kicked beautiful Danny in the gut. He already felt like a louse; he didn't need them judging him. Maybe he needed to put some distance between himself and the situation. "I'm taking a trip to Sacramento, tomorrow. I need to transport a prisoner wanted for robbing a bank to the jail there. Then I might have to spend some time trailing after a few wanted men." His gaze fell on Danny. "Miss Daniella, don't get concerned if you don't see me for a week or so. The sheriff will have everything under control." With one last glance and a wink at Danny, he maneuvered his horse around and galloped away.

"The bastard." The dark mutter came from the back of the watching group.

Danny shook her head at the crowd. "Stop frowning. Everything is perfectly fine. My Caleb is an honorable, decent man. He likes to make his own decisions, and I respect him for it."

The owner of the mercantile patted Danny's shoulder. "So he's not running off to avoid marrying you?"

Danny laughed again and shook her head. "No."

The owner glanced over the other girls surrounding her. "Well, if you aren't upset by what just happened, I guess none of us ought to be, either. I guess you won't be making curtains for Mrs. Faith's bedrooms, after all." He wandered again behind the counter and picked up the bolt of material to return it to its rightful place, still muttering. "Although I must say, most men wait until after they are married to put their foot down on a woman's purchases."

Danny had a twinkle in her eye. "I won't be making any curtains until the deputy agrees, but I think I have another project in mind."

# CHAPTER 2

PLANS...

*D*anny was so engrossed in her sewing project, she barely heard the knocking on the door. The first thing she knew, her golden-haired friend had entered, and a small delicate hand rested on her shoulder.

She jumped a few inches off the bed. "Oh! You startled me," she said, moving the material off to the side.

"I gave up knocking and finally just came in. You were busy," Jeddah explained. "I've never heard of curtains having bodices and sleeves, Danny. Is it a new style?" She tilted her head sideways, grinning as she studied the fabric. "You aren't making window dressings, after all," she blurted out. "That's a beautiful dress. What's the occasion?"

Danny clapped her hands over Jeddah's mouth. Then she rushed to close the bedroom door. "Lower your voice, please. It's a secret."

Jeddah giggled. "A secret? Darlin', people in town are taking bets on when you and Caleb finally set the date. Care to give me a hint? I'm saving up my pocket money to fund a few projects of my own."

"I don't know. Caleb might be upset..." Danny danced from one foot to the other before finally twirling around to face her friend. "Oh, I can't keep it to myself any longer! We are running off to Sacramento as soon as possible." Her eyes were gleaming as she spoke. "Aunt Faith let me borrow her sewing machine, but she thinks I'm making linings for the curtains. It's simple, but I already have it put together except for hemming the sleeves and attaching the skirt. Don't tell her. Danny pulled out the dress and held it up to herself as she gazed happily in the full-length mirror in one corner of the room. "What do you think?"

Jeddah's deep voice was breathy. "Oh, Danny, how romantic! I am so thrilled for you." Jeddah insisted her friend pull on the bodice, and she started attaching the skirt. "Poor Noah will be disappointed not to perform the ceremony. Why don't you two tie the knot here and then go off to Sacramento for a honeymoon?"

"Caleb is quite fed up with the nosey people around town. Today, when I was selecting material for the curtains, he tried to visit with me. The nosey new brides came along, and he ended up losing his temper. He stomped outside and lectured the entire town about crowding us in." She sighed, before continuing in a contented tone of voice and gazing toward the window.

"At first, I started to get upset, thinking he was accusing me of trapping him or something awful. After our talk, earlier, I reminded myself my Caleb loves me. I listened with my heart instead of my pride. After scolding the town's people, he gave me a sweet, knowing wink—and he kissed me—twice, in front of everyone! Then he brought up the topic of going off to Sacramento. He told everyone not to get worried if they didn't see him around."

Jeddah stopped pinning up hem. "Are you certain he meant for you to join him there? Maybe you should ask him to be clear."

Danny wouldn't hear another word. "Now, you sound like me, when you complained to me about Noah. Have a little faith, Jeddah. I think it's so romantic. It will be marvelous, going off with the man I love, taking his last name, enjoying a few days alone, before returning here to Golden River. Now help me pack a few things. I don't want to keep Caleb waiting when he finally shows up."

But Caleb *didn't* show up for dinner that night, and Jeddah kept giving Danny fretful glances. Everyone else did come, however, including Obedience and Tobias.

It was Noah, the town's minister, who finally called attention to the deputy's absence. "I am surprised Caleb isn't at the table," he told the sheriff. "Faith's fried chicken is his favorite meal."

Obie rose as he spoke and rushed from the room. The smell of the fried chicken had gotten to her, after all.

Faith rose. "Stay and eat, Tobias. I'll help her."

The sheriff hesitated but agreed. He was enjoying his food, his first undisturbed meal in a month. "Caleb took off for Sacramento, earlier today. He'd brought in a bank robber who needed transport back to Sacramento. Since he'd brought him in, it only made sense for Caleb to take him back to the city. And I must say, he seemed determined to leave Golden River behind for a bit."

Danny felt her face drain of color, suddenly. "He's already gone?"

The sheriff didn't look up from his plate. "I suggested he head up before nightfall. It's a long ride, and hauling a prisoner will only make it more troublesome."

Sterling, Aunt Faith's husband, coughed a few times, and the sheriff finally stopped eating long enough to look up. Glancing around the table, he wiped his mouth with a napkin and gave Danny an uncomfortable gaze. "I believe, Miss Daniella, he was planning to come calling on you before he left, but I encouraged him to be on his way."

"He was planning on coming to the ranch before he left—and you stopped him?" Danny demanded then realized how rude she sounded. "What I mean to say is," she lowered her voice and blinked, determined to sound more civil, "what makes you think he was going to call on me before leaving?"

Tobias seemed at a loss. When Noah began coughing next, Jeddah started patting his back, and the sheriff appeared more worried about the tickle in Noah's throat than the more pressing matter of Caleb's intent.

Danny's glare transferred from Tobias to Noah and back.

Finally, the sheriff stood up. "I think Obie's calling me. I'd better go check on her."

Danny began pushing back her chair, determined to follow the sheriff until she got her answers. Was Caleb planning on marrying her or not? Had he truly been looking for an opportunity to escape Golden River's meddling? Or had he merely wanted to put some distance between the two of them? She would have her answer, no matter how far she had to follow Tobias.

The sheriff paused at the doorway and raised his hand as if to stall her pursuit. "Yes, as a matter of fact, I am sure Caleb was heading here. I wasn't thinking straight, Danny. I'm sorry. I ordered him to leave for Sacramento with haste. Yes, that's right. I *ordered him*." Hearing Faith's voice coming from the back of the house, he looked over his shoulder. "I'm coming, Obie," he called toward the hall and briefly turned back. "Finish your meal, Daniella, everyone."

Instead of sitting back down, however, she ran toward the stairs and hurried to her room. She could not face the others, again, tonight.

~

The sun had barely risen the next morning, when Daniella slipped out of bed and made her way to the barn. She had packed her trunks the night before and then realized she couldn't take them with her on a horse. Leaving a note under Jeddah's bedroom door, she crept down the hall and out the back. The front door was more tempting, but the noisy spring on the screen door had made her decide to try going out the back way.

She was trying to saddle up a mare, when Henry, one of the ranch hands, found her. It took a bit of sweet talking and a fair bit of fibbing, but she managed to convince him Faith wanted her to go to Sacramento to pick up some special fabric for new curtains.

The young man quickly took the saddle off and, instead, set up the wagon for her as she nervously glanced back at the house. If they were going in the wagon, she could take her trunks with her. Henry didn't ask any questions when she mentioned her trunks. He did raise an eyebrow, when she begged him to retrieve them for her as silently as possible, but nodded. Now, she would only have to make up an excuse to stay in Sacramento, rather than return with him, and hope he would accept it.

Danny allowed him to help her up into the wagon, thankful for his offer to take her. It had been so long since she'd been to Sacramento, she wasn't sure she could remember the way. She paid close attention to the path they traveled through the mountains, giving herself a pep talk the entire way to the city. Henry was known for his quiet demeanor, and she found she was glad. It would give her some time to think on the way.

Caleb loves me, she repeated to herself, more than once. He would have collected me so we could wed in Sacramento, but Tobias ruined his plans. He'll be thrilled I've found my way to his side.

Somehow, the internally spoken words didn't make her feel any better. Had she managed to completely misinterpret what Caleb had said in her ear as he had drawn her closer to him in Golden River? Would he be upset with her for following him?

Danny was determined to end this foolishness, one way or another. When they were face to face, she would know for sure if she and Caleb had a future together. If they did, they could be happily wed before nightfall. If they didn't, she would start a new life, away from both Caleb *and* Golden River.

As far away as possible.

# CHAPTER 3

AND MORE PLANS...

Caleb took off his hat in the afternoon sun and shoved it fiercely down on his head again, glancing at the prisoner who was handcuffed on the horse tethered to his. He thought about the conversation he'd had with Daniella, the morning before, in front of the citizens of Golden River. He hoped she hadn't misunderstood his intentions, and he hoped he hadn't hurt her feelings. He did love her. He cared for her tremendously. He was just tired of being pushed into a box by the entire town. Even Daniella didn't seem as eager as the townspeople were for him to marry her.

His conversation with Tobias came to mind. He hadn't included all of the reasons for the way he felt. Perhaps he should have. It was important to him for Tobias to understand why he felt this way. The sheriff commanded his respect, and he hated the thought of disappointing his boss. More than that, he hated the thought of disappointing Daniella.

"Whoa, Socks. Careful." He slowed his horse, approaching a particularly rocky path through the pass. "Good boy." He looked both ways as they came through. This was an area where outlaws frequented. His right hand rested over his weapon in its holster. He was ready.

But all was quiet. He took the pass easy enough, waiting until they reached the other side before allowing his thoughts to roam free again. Seeing the prisoner glancing at him curiously, he frowned.

"What?"

"You just look disturbed, that's all."

Caleb shook his head. He *was* disturbed. It wasn't just a matter of being shoved toward matrimony by the whole town. A frown increased across his brow as his sandy hair blew in the wind, and he shoved it further under his hat, remembering the way things had been at home when he was a lad. His father had passed away several years earlier, and his mother, a strong woman, managed to work various jobs to put food on the table. It had disturbed Caleb terribly to see her come in from working so hard, and he had put his young foot down. He'd quit school and gone to work, insisting his mother go back to keeping house and let him do the harder work which would bring in enough to keep the household going. Ranching, he'd understood. He could do it.

At first, his mother had disagreed. She wanted him to finish school. But a conversation with the teacher had convinced her Caleb already knew all she had to teach him. In the end, his mother had agreed to let him quit.

Taking off to find work on neighboring farms and ranches, Caleb faithfully kept sending back money to help provide for his three sisters and two brothers. He'd done it for several years, until one day his mother had sent a letter. Out of the blue, she wanted him to come back home. She had met a fine, wealthy gentleman, and they were going to be wed.

Caleb had felt a combination of guilt and relief. He'd made the trip home. His step-father had been a kind man, and it seemed as if he would take good care of the family. Caleb had stayed only long enough to embrace them all and say goodbye and had gone on his way. His mother had promised to write, and he'd made sure to keep in touch with her.

This was the time for him to be on his own. He'd planned for it; he'd waited for it.

"You're deep, deputy." When Caleb raised a brow, the prisoner continued. "This is dangerous territory, and you're not paying attention. Should I?"

A scowl consumed Caleb's brow, and he urged Socks into a gallop. "I'm paying attention. Mind your own business," he threw back, ending the conversation, once and for all.

But his brain didn't stop its whirling. Only once, a year after leaving home, had he entertained the thought of marriage. The boss' daughter had caught his eye, a pretty young lady with golden hair and eyes the color of the sky. He'd had dreams of wedding her, and they consumed him. But her father had other ideas, and when the news was announced that she was soon to be married to someone else, Caleb lost his vision and his heart. Never again, would he fall for a girl so hard. He'd see to it.

"Look out!" A shout from the prisoner jerked him back to reality.

"Easy, boy," he said gently in response, when Socks reared upward. This was rattler territory, and Caleb watched carefully. The prisoner was right.

"Pay attention, Matthews," he ground out, between his teeth, low enough so the prisoner couldn't hear.

"Hey, buddy. At least, let me have my weapon, so I can protect myself."

Caleb glared at him. "Shut up. I should have shot you on sight when I found you behind the bank."

His prisoner, realizing his tactic didn't work, made a face and became quiet for the rest of the journey. But Caleb was more alert to their surroundings.

It was after the wedding of the boss' daughter that different kinds of dreams had entered his head. The news of the gold rush had worked its way east. It had seduced him into believing it was possible to get rich quick. The people who worked alongside him at the last ranch tried to convince him it was a fool's dream, but Caleb's stubborn pride had gotten in the way of logic. He'd looked them in the eye, and straightening his shoulders, said the words that haunted him, even now.

"No one's going to tell me what I can or can't do. Ever. Again." With that statement, he'd headed west to Golden River and worked the mines until his good sense finally caught up with his greed. He could almost hear everyone back home mocking his foolish decision. Things had begun to get tough, until Tobias approached him one day and offered to hire him on as deputy.

The trail widened out a bit under Socks' feet, and he knew they were on the last leg of the journey. He urged Socks a little faster.

He'd liked Golden River. He was happy here. For the first time, he was free to come and go as he pleased. Hell, if being a deputy in Golden River got too mundane, he could pack up and move anywhere he wanted, do anything he chose. At least, he'd felt that way in the beginning.

Then he'd gone and fallen for Daniella Abcott. Damn. How and why, he wasn't sure, but the ornery little vixen called to him in a way no other woman ever had. He thought of the night, a few weeks before the sheriff and Obedience married, that all three of the ladies had sneaked out of the house in response to the bawl of their calf, Buster. The girls hadn't hesitated. They went after two of the most dangerous rustlers in the territory, and when he'd gotten his hands on Daniella again, he'd spanked the daylights out of her. Acting before thinking was one thing he'd have to work with her on. Hopefully, he could correct that before the wedding. But deep down, he wasn't completely sure she'd ever learn.

He wouldn't leave Golden River for good, not as long as Danny was there, and he knew it.

The road smoothed out as they approached Sacramento, deep dark twinkling brown eyes appearing before his vision. Hair pulled back in a ribbon at the back of her head tried unsuccessfully to contain long dark curls that trailed down her back, and dimples more pronounced on the left than the right teased him.

He couldn't seem to get her out of his mind. Wishing he'd grabbed her up and brought her with him to Sacramento, he shook his head.

Daniella would just have to understand this was his decision and respect it. She was a smart young lady, although a might stubborn and too quick to act without thinking things through. But she'd learn.

He set his jaw. He would help her work on those flaws *before* they wed. It would make life together so much easier on them both.

~

Sacramento was a bustling place; luckily, the jail wasn't far inside the city limits, and his first stop was to drop off the prisoner. The sheriff was amazed at Caleb's delivering him and offered him a job. But Caleb politely refused and went on his way.

Just down the street, he could see the hotel, with the hostler around back. Guiding Socks up in front of the walk, he made arrangements to have him fed and watered and turned to come back outside. It was late, and he was tired. Finding a meal and getting a room was next, and he dropped his things into it before making a trip down the street toward the saloon.

Sauntering inside the swinging doors, he let his eyes adjust to the dim light. There were no empty tables, and he moved to the bar and took a seat.

It didn't help. Two drinks later, and he gave up and moved back to the room.

All he could see was Daniella's darling little face.

Damn.

~

Caleb slept late the next morning, after tossing most of the night. Daniella had continually crept into his dreams. In the first one, she'd found her way to Sacramento, and the white material he'd taken from her grasp the day before had been turned into a wedding dress. In the next, he'd come into the room to find her wearing only her shift, her soft curves giving it a delicious shape. The dream of her lying in his bed, naked, tormented him throughout the rest of the night.

When he at last blinked and opened his eyes, he realized he was staring at the light from the window. It must be mid-morning, at least. Running his fingers through his hair, he sat up and decided to head downstairs and scout out the town. He was in no mood to return to Golden River today.

Outside, however, he stopped with an abrupt halt, staring. A young lady had stepped across the street in front of him, moving in the opposite direction. Her provocative sway nearly caused him to go after her.

"Daniella?"

She hadn't heard.

He stood there for a moment. Surely, he was losing his mind. A growl formed deep in his throat as he considered catching up with her and taking her by the shoulders.

But the next thing that happened convinced him he was sane, after all. He saw Henry, the younger ranch hand, getting into the wagon. Faith's wagon.

Within three or four strides, he reached it.

"Henry?"

The young man looked relieved. "Oh! Deputy Matthews, I'm so glad to see you. I didn't quite know what to do."

Caleb glanced toward the restaurant in the hotel a few doors down. Daniella—if it was indeed Daniella, had now disappeared inside. He jammed both hands in his pockets and cocked his head to one side. "Explain."

"Miss Daniella talked me into bringing her here, this morning, to do some shopping for Faith."

Caleb's eyes narrowed. "Oh, she did, did she?"

"Yes. I thought it was odd that she asked me to get her trunks for her. But when she got here, she thanked me and said she was meeting you but not to tell anyone. I wasn't sure where to find you, but I didn't feel like I could leave her here."

Caleb could feel his pulse at his throat, pounding. He stood there a moment, trying to figure out what to do. A tricky one, that girl. He had half a mind to go after her, grab her and put her across his knee, and then put her back in the wagon and send her home.

But first, they needed to talk. And she would do her talking face down, if he had anything to do with it.

Finally, he nodded. "Go ahead and leave her, Henry. I'll take care of getting her back home, but it may not be today. Tell Faith and Sterling not to worry. And Obedience and Tobias."

Henry frowned but finally nodded toward him. "She went to the hotel to get something to eat. I took her trunks in and left them at the desk."

"I see. Thanks, Henry. See you back at the ranch in a few days."

Henry lifted a hand in a wave goodbye and disappeared, leaving Caleb standing there with his hands still in his pockets, his jaw pulsing and his mouth flattened into a straight line. He felt the sense of irritation he'd felt yesterday in town when he was talking to Tobias all over again. Anger welled up in him.

So, little Danny had left home and come to the big city of Sacramento. He shook his head. How did she think she would manage? Suppose he hadn't seen her? What did she intend to do? He let out a sigh and strode toward the hotel.

Approaching the desk with hat in hand, he waited for the clerk to turn toward him. He took a moment to glance into the dining room. He could see her, in the corner, looking over the menu. Every moment or so, she glanced up with large, frightened eyes, as if she didn't know what to do.

"May I help, sir?"

He nodded. "Yes. Caleb Matthews, room three fourteen. My..." he paused, stammering.

The woman was looking back at him as if she knew what he was going to say, and the difference in their last names would tell her he and Daniella weren't married. He frowned at her.

"My wife will be joining me here, today. Her first name is Daniella." Forcing himself to give her a wide grin, he continued. "She'll probably introduce herself as Daniella Abcott. We haven't been married long. When she checks in, you can tell her I'll be detained for a bit, but I'll be back. I'll settle her meals with the room."

She looked at him oddly. "Yes, sir. When she comes, I'll see she gets a key."

"Thanks, ma'am."

He glanced once more into the dining room as he turned to leave.

Daniella was staring straight at him, her eyes growing wide. But Caleb wasn't about to attempt a conversation with her right now. He nodded, jamming his hat back down on his head, and left.

Standing on the walk, he looked around. Three doors down to the left was the saloon, and he headed in that direction.

He needed a stiff drink. And he needed to think, before he had this conversation with little miss Daniella.

# CHAPTER 4

CONFUSION...

*D*aniella could not believe her eyes. Caleb had left her behind. He had seen her, stared her straight in the eyes, and turned and walked away. Self-doubt settled like a stone in her stomach. Had she made a horrible mistake, following him here? Maybe the sheriff had been wrong when he suggested Caleb had meant to come for her.

She tried to settle her bill for the light meal but was promptly informed a gentleman had already paid for it. Looking at the waiter strangely, she rushed back to the hotel's front door to see if Henry might still be in town. She paled. If he was, she would have to come up with a reason for needing to return home with him. Quite frankly, she was at a loss.

Stopping just inside the door, she looked up and down the street. There was no sign of Caleb now. And none at all of Henry. Both he and the wagon were gone. She turned back toward the desk, to try to decide what to do about her trunks.

Daniella didn't realize she was muttering until the lady at the desk addressed her.

"Did you say something, Mrs. Matthews?"

"Mrs. Matthews..." Danny paused, the thought of chasing down Henry temporarily forgotten. "My name is Abcott. Daniella Abcott."

The woman let out a delightful chuckle. "Your husband mentioned you have trouble remembering your married name."

"My husband?" Danny wondered if she was suffering from heat stroke. This entire day was turning into a nightmare. This morning, she had set out for the city, hoping with all her heart she would be wedding the man of her dreams. But Caleb had walked away from her just now, instead of rejoicing to find her here. Maybe the sheriff and Jeddah had both been wrong about his intentions toward her. She would die of humiliation if anyone in Golden River heard about this.

"You two must be freshly married, my dear. Mr. Matthews said to tell you he would be detained. He must have some important business to take care of. Not to worry. I assured him I'd give you a key to your room, as well. I'll have someone bring up your trunks in a moment. Your room is the last one down the hall on the left—top floor."

Hope welled up, replacing the despair in the pit of Daniella's stomach. "My husband, Mr. Matthews, Caleb Matthews?" She hoped the desperation in her tone wasn't too obvious.

The lady behind the desk laughed good-naturedly. "Go ahead and say it aloud, my dear. It will help you embrace your new role."

"Pardon?" Danny asked, baffled.

"Your new name, of course. Tell the world you are Mrs. Caleb Matthews, new bride and proud wife."

A huge smile consumed Danny's face, her eyes twinkling with joy. Caleb *did* mean to marry her. He even rented a room for them to spend their first night as husband and wife. Images of him rushing off to track down someone to marry them filled her thoughts. She wanted to hug the woman who handed her the room key. "Mrs. Caleb Matthews does have a wonderful ring to it, don't you think? I'll just go upstairs and get ready for his return."

Danny ascended the stairway with a spring in her step. Her

joyous smile reached her eyes as she turned left on the top floor, the key clasped tightly in her hand. She paused just outside the door and managed to get it in the lock. But she had difficulty opening it due to the trembling of her hands.

Her breath hitched as she gave it a shove. Inside, she looked around. It was a fairly large room, with high ceilings, and a high bed with a stepstool beside it. Waiting until the man came and delivered her trunks, she dropped a coin into his hand and closed the door after him. She gulped and climbed up onto the bed. It was even higher than the one in her room at Aunt Faith's house, and she had to resort to using the stepstool provided.

"Well, Daniella? What have you gotten yourself into?" Her voice echoed in the big room. But as she waited, she sighed. Climbing back down, she moved to the window. As big as Sacramento was, ministers or judges must be hard to come by. It was taking him a long time.

But something caught her eye as she stared out the window. A ladies' ready to wear shop was directly across the street, and an idea popped into her mind, accompanied by a huge smile. She turned to see herself in the long mirror in the corner of the room as the smile grew wider.

Quickly, she grabbed her reticule and let herself out of the room, locking it behind her and hurrying down the steps.

THINKING...

Caleb sat at the bar, staring straight ahead and wondering how long he'd been there. She had actually followed him here? He shook his head.

*Of course, she had followed him here.* She was Daniella, after all. She was determined to have her way—Daniella's way. How could he expect otherwise?

He felt something brush up against his side and turned. A

woman, in a silky dress that barely covered her bosom, was rubbing her hand lightly up and down his arm.

"Hello, Deputy." She fingered the shiny badge on his vest. "Could I interest you in a dance?"

Realizing, for the first time, there was a fiddle playing in the background, he frowned. "No, ma'am. Too drunk to dance. And too irrit...irrit..." He paused. "Too angry to talk."

"Ah. A shame, a handsome man like you. If you change your mind, I'll be here." Her petticoats made a swishing sound as she moved away. He realized he had failed to even notice what she looked like. All he could see in front of his eyes was a mischievous little face surrounded by dark curls with twinkling brown eyes. And most of the time, a dimple which lit up her face beside a luscious little mouth. When she was truly happy, both dimples showed. When she was full of mischief, only one. He wondered if she realized how easy she was to read.

He slid a few coins across the bar and nodded to the barkeep before standing to his feet. It was necessary to grab hold of the bar as the room swayed around him. Blinking at the lights, he decided it was time to make it to their room and give Daniella a piece of his mind. A scowl plastered its way across his mouth. He'd been thinking of what to say to her all afternoon.

Problem was, right now, he couldn't remember what it was.

Any of it.

~

WAITING...

As evening settled and there was no sign of her groom, she began to grow worried. Their room faced the main road into town. She watched anxiously as street lamps were lit, sure Caleb would be approaching any minute. She'd only been gone a few moments this afternoon; surely, Caleb hadn't come back with the minister and left again. A small palm made its way to her face.

No, she decided. Caleb wouldn't have done that. Tonight, *would* be her wedding night. The thought both thrilled and terrified her. Thrilled, because she wanted to be Caleb's wife more than anything in the world, and terrified, because she did not have the faintest idea of how to please a man. Her mother had borne lots of children, all boys, except for Daniella. But she had never taken the time to discuss how a person got into such a condition with her daughter.

"Oh, Mama, why didn't you ever talk to me about these things?" she whispered into the emptiness.

Glancing around her in the dim light, she took in the room, studying its detail. The lamps were anchored to the wall, and she lit them quickly and stood there, wondering what to do next. Suppose Caleb didn't return?

Sighing, she began tapping her slipper-clad toe on the braided rug on which she stood. Either Caleb was equally worried about the coming coupling, thus, trying to stall, or he was not all that eager to bed her.

Her heart sank. Was it possible he didn't want her, after all? If not, why tell the woman at the desk they were already married? Why pay for her meal? Why look her in the eye, when he could easily have pretended she wasn't there at all?

She moved toward the trunks she'd brought with her and began to unpack, thoroughly confused.

∼

SEEING HIM...

Loud singing erupted from down the way, and Daniella opened the window, sticking her head out to investigate. To her amazement, the crooner was none other than her future husband.

"Caleb Matthews, what has gotten into you?" she yelled out before she thought better of it. She looked around for a second man. If her future mate had found the time to go drinking, surely, he had managed to secure someone to perform the ceremony.

Caleb stumbled to a stop near the middle of the road. His eyes lifted to where she leaned down toward him, and he reached up, tipping his hat in her direction. "Well, hello there, you...you bossy little mail order brat, you." He paused, slurring his words as he swayed again. "Be still, would you? I see you found your room."

She was frowning now. "You mean *our* room? Yes, I found it."

"Good of you to wait—up for me. You and I are about to have a very long, serious dis—" He paused. "Dis—" He frowned again. "Talk." He looked around as if he needed something to hold on to and managed to right himself.

Danny called down to him, "Sir, you seem to have trouble staying upright. I doubt you are capable of finding your way to our room, much less participating in a *discussion*." So much for her concern about their wedding night. She would be lucky to get him up to their room before he passed out. Oh, well, the lady at the front desk thought they were already wed. Taking care of making it official would have to wait until the next day. "Shall I come down and help you, Caleb?"

"You. Shall. *Not!*" he announced and almost tripped over his right foot with his left. He shook his head from side to side, before glaring up at her again. "Are you hanging out that window with nothing on?"

"I am not," she shouted back. "It's my shift. I didn't want to wrinkle my dress before the ceremony, so I took it off and hung it up. It would seem it was a wasted effort, because *someone* forgot to bring a preacher back with him."

The sound of another window opening startled Danny, and she ducked back inside.

"Both of you stop yelling!" a male voice growled from below. "Some of us are trying to sleep."

Caleb took off his hat and gave a smart salute, and Danny started giggling. Staying upset at Caleb was difficult. She'd loved him with all her heart, from the moment she'd laid eyes on him, swimming naked in the river. She watched her love shove his hat back down hard, over his head. He marched toward the hotel, only swaying every other step or so.

She pulled the window to and jerked the curtains closed, stepping quickly back. He would be in the room before she knew it. Should she put her dress back on? She glanced at the sheer lacy nightgown she'd purchased earlier that afternoon. It lay discreetly in a nearby corner, draped delicately over a chair. She had splurged when she purchased it, but after all, this would be the first night she'd share with Caleb, right?

She clasped the nightgown in her hands. But before she could remove her shift to pull it on over her head, the lock on the door was turned, and Caleb stormed inside. Danny realized he was angry, now that his face was not shadowed in darkness. The last time she had seen that expression had been at the ranch. He'd given her a terrible spanking for sneaking out in the night in search of rustlers. Her hands instinctively reached back to shield her backside, and the dress she had been holding slipped to the floor.

Caleb's eyes dropped to her chest. Her breasts strained against her thin shift as her heart raced. She watched as his countenance changed from fury to something more confusing. He kicked the door shut behind him with the heel of his boot before turning the lock. When he faced her and started in her direction, she took a step back.

"Son of a b—" One eyebrow rose, and he looked as if he'd forgotten what he'd planned to say. "It wasn't a dream, after all?" He shook his head. "Daniella Abcott, just being around you makes my legs weak." His words were slightly slurred but easy to understand. "And how the hell am I supposed to control you, when I can't even control myself? Especially with you standing there naked and perfect?"

*Perfect?* Danny gasped. Something stirred deep within her, and she felt herself go damp in places she never had before. "Oh, Caleb. No one has ever said anything so wonderful to me." She took a step toward him, ready to throw herself in his arms.

Suddenly, she stopped. "I've always felt as if I've been relegated to second choice," she whispered.

"Second?" His husky voice, along with his hungry eyes, made her feel lightheaded as he mumbled. "Man would have to be blind."

She gulped and moved toward him slowly. "Caleb Matthews, I love you. So much." All worries about not knowing how to please him vanished, suddenly. He made her feel so special, so loved, she was emboldened to try just about anything. Reaching up on her tiptoes, she pressed her lips awkwardly against his.

At first, he didn't seem inclined to return her affections. He actually stiffened.

"Caleb?" Her eyes grew large, her voice tremulous. Was it possible he was new to this, too? She looked up into dark, hungry eyes, uncertain what to do next.

Wondering if she could soothe his concerns, she reached for his large hand, taking it between her much smaller ones. She pulled it up and rested it against her chest through the thin material, over her beating heart. She knew he could feel it; her heart was pounding so rapidly. As she held his hard palm in place, she spoke in gentle tones. "I am as nervous as you are, Caleb. But there is nothing to be ashamed of. I want it as much as you do."

His fingers pulled out of hers, but before she could protest, his hand lowered to cup her breast. His thumb reached up to rub against her nipple, sending glorious shivers down her body. She reached for his other hand, as if begging him to caress the other side. He groaned, his head lowering to take the tip of one breast inside his mouth. He sucked sharply, and the thin material of her shift became translucent when he released it. Her dark pink nipple was pebbling as it clung to the damp cloth.

Caleb yanked at the material, almost ripping it in his haste to remove it. It came over her head and ended up thrown across the room. Stepping back and drinking in every inch of her frame, he muttered, almost as if to himself, "If I were a gentleman, I would turn around and head back to the bar until morning."

"And leave me all alone in this strange hotel room?" she cooed, her voice sounding coy. Were they playing a game? She lifted her lips upward, continuing. "A gentleman would finish what he started." As she spoke, Danny recalled his stubborn pride. He did seem a bit touchy on doing things in his own time. No doubt, he wanted to wait until they were properly married before coming together the first time.

Blowing a few strands of hair from her face, Danny realized she would have to come to terms with that small flaw in Caleb's character. The future would be full of times she would have to settle for doing things on his time. A wicked smile crossed her lips. In his current state, she had little doubt she could override his stubborn need for control. What was the harm of enjoying this little victory before settling into a life of submission to her husband?

She strolled over to the bed, making sure she gave her exaggerated sway, and slowly climbed up onto it, easing herself onto the mattress. Did she have the courage to tempt fate? Danny forced herself to give it a shot. Her hand reached up slowly, and she started mimicking the way he had touched her breast. Though not as exciting as when he had done it, she found herself thrilled by the way his eyes locked on her. "We both want this, Caleb. Why deny ourselves, just because the official wedding hasn't taken place?"

Caleb was swaying from the effects of the whiskey he'd consumed, looking as if he was not at all convinced. "Are you sure, Daniella?" he demanded.

She nodded, proud of herself for getting him to agree so readily. Maybe there was hope for the future, after all. With time, Caleb might mellow on the subject of who was in control. Danny watched him try to work the buttons of his shirt and giggled when he couldn't quite manage the trick. Buttons popped loudly, shooting across the room when he got frustrated and ripped his shirt off. His belt, however, cooperated, and he didn't have to destroy his pants, too.

Danny's giggling abruptly ceased as she got her first real glimpse of a man's member, straight and stiff. She began to panic.

How did men manage to hide such a thick rod in their breeches? She'd seen him naked, but it hadn't seemed so large then.

Was he thinking he could try putting something so big inside of her body? It would never fit. Her hands stilled over her breast, and he scowled.

"Don't stop, Daniella." It was an order. "Show me how you want to be touched." Caleb slowly crossed the room, his hard body becoming much harder to ignore.

Danny turned her crimson face away, her eyes dropping to her chest. The sight of her darkened pink nipples, squeezed tightly between her own fingers, shocked her.

"So, you want a less *gentle* touch." His slurred words caused her to glance up into his eyes again. He crawled over her on the bed, his large frame looming above her, his muscular thighs straddling her hips. Caleb's hand reached up to replace one of hers. Because it was larger, he was able to clasp more area. Her nipple peeked out between his rough grasp, and he reached down to suck it between his teeth.

She braced herself for the pain but only found unbelievable pleasure. The harder he nibbled, the stronger the ripples coursed through her body. Her heart seemed to feel hollow, suddenly, as she responded to him without reservation. Soon, she was so damp, Danny feared she might have accidently relieved herself. To her horror, Caleb choose that moment to reach lower down her body and explore. He sucked in his breath when he found her drenched. Mortified, she wanted to cry.

"You're already so wet for me, my girl." He buried his head in the crook of her neck. "I thought it would take a long time to ready you to take me."

"Wet is good?" Danny asked. Perhaps she had not ruined everything, after all.

"It's perfect. *You're* perfect." Leaning down on his elbows, he took her face into his hands and stared down into her eyes. "You sure this is really what you want?" Caleb shook his head, as if trying to rid himself of the effects of his drinking. If he succeeded, Danny had no doubt he would reconsider going through with things.

"Are you sure I am wet enough?" she managed to ask, her face going scarlet with what she was about to suggest. "Maybe you should check again…with your fingers…just to make sure."

She watched his face tense as if to reject the suggestion, but his hands could not seem to stop themselves from seeking her warmth. He moved lower on the bed, roughly parting her legs wide so he could see her response. But when his head found its way between her legs, she started to stiffen. She attempted to close her legs tightly, but his grip on her thighs prevented her from it. His lips begin tasting her without even pausing.

Danny gasped as his tongue drove her out of her mind, making her dizzy. The faster it moved, the more relaxed her legs became, until they touched the mattress. She had just rested her hands on his wavy blond head when it happened. Something was building. Something she could not control. When her entire body began tensing up, she felt as if someone had pushed her off a high cliff. But instead of falling, she was flying across the valley, weightless, the rapid beat of her heart lifting her higher and higher on each wave of bliss. It seemed to go on forever.

~

A wide grin spread across Caleb's mouth as he moved upward directly over her face. "If you weren't wet enough before," he announced, "you will be now." He moved his hips over her body again, pulling her legs up and around him. Then he slowly guided himself toward her center.

She gasped, and her eyes grew wide as she stared up into his face.

He leaned down again, over her. "Listen to me, young lady," he growled as he forced her to meet his gaze. "I've had enough of your attempts at control. It's time you listened. Hear me?"

Her eyes still enormous in her small face, she nodded, and he spoke once again, more forcefully. "One more time. Are you sure you want this? Take a moment. Think about it."

Daniella didn't speak, and he didn't allow her to move. He had her trapped under him and caged quite effectively. Even in his inebriated state, he was determined to make her listen to him.

She blinked and nodded. "I want this."

"You're sure?"

"Yes." It was a frightened whisper.

Caleb stared down into her eyes, frowning. *Get up*, he ordered himself. *Be the gentleman she thinks you are. Leave the room.*

Why couldn't he make himself do it? Instead, he stayed, keeping his eyes on her face, looking for any signs of discomfort or fear—of rejection.

There were none.

He moved his hips toward hers and entered her small channel, watching as her eyes stayed on his. Still, there was no sign of pain, and this time, he leaned forward, into her.

He paused. Something seemed to be blocking his efforts.

Danny seemed fretful. "I *thought* it might be too large to fit." She sounded heartbroken, and Caleb leaned down to kiss her petulant little mouth.

He tightened his fists into her hair, holding her still. "Do you really love me, Danny girl?" he asked, planting another kiss her forehead.

"Oh, Caleb, of course," she whispered without hesitation. "*You know I do.*"

"Remember that. Because, in a few seconds, I'm going to hurt you. But—it only hurts the first time."

"What do you mean, it only hurts the—" Her gasp reached him as she prepared to scream. "Sto—" She wasn't able to finish before he clapped his hand firmly over her mouth, silencing her.

"Shhh. The hotel will be beating down our doors. I'm s-sorry, Daniella." He watched, concerned as her eyes closed, and waited for her to open them again.

∽

*D*anny kept her eyes tightly closed, feeling as if something inside her had been dislodged. For a second or two, stars flashed before her eyes. The delightful sensation of flying had disappeared, and she felt as if she was plummeting to the ground quickly.

"Quiet..." His voice was quiet, as well. Caleb stoked her hair and whispered sweet words into her ear. Even if they were slurred, they were soothing. He was buried deep inside her. The pain had eased, but she still felt as if she was being stretched.

"Daniella? If you're all right, I'll move my hand."

Slowly, she nodded and looked up into his face, unable now to take her eyes from his.

Finding her voice, she tried to explain away her response. "Are you sure I was wet enough before you began? Caleb, this doesn't feel quite right."

He shifted his hips, slowly withdrawing from her. Danny was relieved but tried not to show it. She didn't want to hurt his feelings. Could a couple have a happy marriage without taking part in this act? She was pondering just that when he thrust inward once again.

He seemed to be waiting on her reply, and she nodded.

Once again, he withdrew, but only for a few seconds before thrusting deeper inside. The number of times he moved assured Danny he knew exactly what he was doing. He was making deep, grunting noises now. At first, she thought he might be in pain, but then she concluded he was about to leap off his own cliff and fly, just as she had earlier.

Wanting to help him along, she lifted her hips a bit, accepting his thrusts. Her efforts had him growling words of praise, "That's it, little one. Take me deep."

She complied and was shocked when she started feeling herself tighten against another oncoming wave. Pushing up faster to meet him, she kept pace with him, urging him on. Both let out a hoarse shout when they surrendered to it.

An exhausted Caleb barely managed to shift his weight until he was no longer on top of her. He pulled her close to his body, cradling her form against his as they drifted off into a peaceful sleep.

CHAPTER 5

SECOND THOUGHTS...

The lamps in the room were still lit when Danny awakened, close to dawn, the urge to relieve herself outweighing the glory of staying in Caleb's embrace. She slipped out of bed and quietly found the chamber pot, keeping an eye on him as he slept, his handsome face reflecting the shadows of the lamp light.

Such a handsome face it was, so full of character, even in peaceful sleep. She turned away and approached the bath stand, deciding to wash up a bit before returning to bed. The cool water felt soothing on her tender skin as she cleaned away the sticky residue of lovemaking.

Silently, she scowled, inwardly groaning with frustration. She studied the cloth she was using, realizing it had a red tinge to it. What a time for her menses to arrive, she thought. Her body must be off balance, because she was supposed to be closer to mid cycle, rather than near the end. How disappointed would Caleb be when he discovered their honeymoon was over before they even officially got married? But there was no help for it. At least, they had the memories of last night to look back on.

Slipping back toward the bed, she watched as Caleb shifted position. He was now facing the door, nothing covering his glorious body from view. She paused, staring, and smiling. "It's okay to look," she whispered to herself. "After last night, there is nothing to hide from each other."

Danny's eyes started at his head and worked their way down. Would she ever get used to seeing him this way? It seemed so sinfully thrilling. His chest was hard and his belly flat. She longed to touch the skin there. Was it smooth, or did the trail of light hair give it a coarse feel? A frown marred her lips when her glance settled a bit lower. While still impressive, she recalled his member being larger. It had stood straight out then, but now hung to the side.

His light snoring gave her courage to move closer. She cautiously reached one finger over to touch it. It was much softer now, but it bobbed and started growing stiff with contact. She yanked her hand away and rushed to the other side of the bed to climb in.

She paused abruptly, the stain of red halting her efforts. She had stained the hotel's sheet—*how dreadful!* If Caleb wasn't sleeping so contently on the bed, she'd have pulled them off to try cleaning up.

Realization came slowly as she stood there, her eyes wide. The blood was not from her monthly. Last night, Caleb's huge member had felt like it ripped something inside of her.

*Oh, God.* She knew it was too big. Would she bleed like this every time they loved each other? How much blood could a person lose before they died?

No. *Calm down*, she ordered herself.

Her mother had given birth many times and survived. That implied she had not bled to death from participating in the activity which begot children. Begot children? Danny froze in terror. She knew Caleb meant to marry her, today, but what if something unforeseen happened? What if he got called away and had to leave her behind? Then she would have to return to Golden River as an unwed mother. The shame would be too much to bear.

They had to marry, and they had to do it *now*. Waiting was unthinkable.

Easing back around the bed, she searched for the dress she'd taken off yesterday. She had no desire to go rummaging through her trunks with Caleb in the room. She pulled it on over her head, watching him as he slept, unaware that she was about to leave and go find a priest, herself.

"*Wait!*" an insistent voice said in her ear. It was her conscience; she'd heard it before. "Talk to Caleb. Let him decide what to do about this. Didn't he give you shelter for the night? Didn't he provide for your meal downstairs? Hasn't he taken care of you and protected you up to now? Trust him!"

Daniella shook her head vehemently against the voice. *No.* She would not wake him to trouble him with this. Buttoning her dress, she decided to take matters into her own hands yet again. Caleb might enjoy setting his own time frames, but after last night, she could not afford to wait until he decided to follow through.

She would go and hunt for someone to marry them.

She let herself out, glad to see there was no one at the desk. She could hear noises in the back, where the kitchen must be, and decided someone must be working on cooking breakfast.

Standing outside, she glanced up and down the street. From here, she could see the saloon, with its swinging doors. It was still, now. Caleb had probably been sitting inside those doors all afternoon, yesterday. But turning the other way, she saw lamplight through a series of windows.

She moved toward it. A small chapel stood not far down the street. An elderly priest was holding early mass for a few parishioners, but no one noticed her as she slipped in and sat near the back, taking part in the services.

She was still there, praying for God to forgive her brazen behavior the night before and help Caleb accept her need to rush the wedding, when the priest found her there, later. When she raised her head to look around, everyone had gone.

"Lass, is there something I can counsel ye on? I'm Father McKnight." He spoke in a musical accent Danny had never encountered before.

She finally found the courage to meet his face. "Oh, Father, I am hoping you will be willing to help me, for I have made a grave error in judgement."

The man gave her a gentle nod. "Go on now, explain the trouble you'd be having."

Danny was twisting her hands in her lap, but she made an attempt. "I'm from Golden River. Actually, a ranch just outside town." Finding the words was harder than she thought it would be.

"I'd have taken your way of talking to mean you were from back east. I had a wee parish near New York before coming out here."

Danny tried to smile and be friendly. "So that's what a New York accent sounds like? I heard it was different."

"Ah, lass, me accent is Scotch-Irish. 'Tis where I was born, but enough about me history. I want to help ye with yer own." He was frowning at her. "Last heard, Golden River had only men, save a woman outside town who owned a ranch. Yes, lass, word travels here from all over. Where did ye come from?'

"Father." She was unable to still her hands. "I *am* from back east. I answered a mail order bride advertisement. It said the men in Golden River want to turn the area into a family town." After finally getting started, Danny found it easier to talk to the holy man. He wasn't overly harsh as her priest back home had been.

"Don't be telling me you ran away from home. Surely, you won't have put such a horrible worry on your dear parents' hearts."

"Oh, no, sir. I came with their blessings. I even found the perfect man, one I could not only love but also respect. We are here in Sacramento, to be married."

The priest patted her hand as it rested on the kneeler. "What's worrying ye then, lass? Bring the young man by. I'd be more than honored to help ye out. We'll need a witness, of course. Do ye have anyone in mind, or shall I try to get someone?"

"Father, I need to go to confession before I take my vows. And, well, I also need help to get my groom to cooperate with the ceremony. I don't think he's Catholic, you see. In Golden River, we only have one minister. He's my best friend's intended, so I am fairly certain he is not Catholic, either."

He leaned back, folding his arms. "Marrying outside the faith is frowned upon, lass. The fact that the young man needs help agreeing to show up to the altar gives me pause, too. It might be wise to put off the ceremony until I have a chance to counsel ye both. Maybe we can make a Catholic out of him yet."

"We can't put off the wedding, Father. It's imperative we are married today." Danny began wringing her hands together. "We already…last night…I assumed he was coming back to the hotel with someone to marry us. He registered the room in the name of Mr. and Mrs. Caleb Matthews, so I don't think I was being too forward. But he showed up drunk, and there was no one there to perform a ceremony."

"He took advantage of you, lass?" The priest's voice grew dark suddenly.

"Oh, no, Father. If anything, I am responsible for this entire situation." Danny could not allow the holy man to think poorly of Caleb. She needed his cooperation, not his censorship.

"Take me to this man ye seek to wed, lass. No, the time for words is over. I want to see exactly what type of situation I'll be dealing with." He marched her out the chapel, down the road, and into the hotel as if she were a wayward child being sent home to face the consequences of her misbehavior.

The woman at the front desk looked up in alarm. "Father McKnight, is everything all right? Mrs. Matthews, is there a problem the hotel should know about?"

"No, Miss Mildred," the priest called back with a wave, forcing a more tranquil expression on his face. "I just discovered the dear lady is Catholic and canna resist the urge to make friends. She's taking me up to introduce me to—"

The woman frowned at his pause. "Mr. Caleb Matthews, her husband?"

"Oh, aye, Mr. Matthews. Anytime you feel like converting, let me know, Miss Mildred. I've heard yer angel voice floating out the doors of the Methodist church. Our own wee choir is a bit lacking. Good morning to ye."

The priest bade Danny to give him the room key, and he unlocked the door. Caleb was still snoozing away, his body on full display. She tried to rush over and pull up the covers to spare his modesty, but the priest ordered her to stay in place. "Mr. Caleb Matthews, it's time for ye to wake up and face the consequences of yer own sinful actions."

At the booming words, Caleb shot up to a sitting position. Danny saw him send a hand to his right hip to grab something, probably his gun. It wasn't there. Then he appeared to decide to let his eyes adjust to the glare, trying to assess the situation. Her Caleb was a brilliant man. So smart. So logical. Eventually, he would be bound to overlook this little rushed ceremony, wouldn't he? Perhaps in a year or two, Danny doubted either one of them would even mention the subject.

"Anyone care to explain what's going on?" Caleb asked, his eyes locking on hers, his hand reaching up to rub his temples.

"This innocent child just showed up in my chapel wrought with guilt." The priest acted more like the fire and brimstone version Danny remembered from back home.

"Wrought is a bit strong, Father. *Confused,* maybe," she whispered, but the priest paid her no heed.

"Did ye, or did ye not, claim this young woman's innocence last night?" The priest stepped closer to Caleb, and Danny tried to rush to place herself between them. The priest started to pull her behind his back, but Caleb was faster. He was on his feet and grabbed her, using his own naked frame to shield her. But the expression of pain on his face suggested it was not a pleasant action.

He squared off with the intruder. "Look, mister. I don't know who the hell you think you are, but whatever happened in this room is between Miss Abcott and me."

Danny gasped and chided him. "Don't say hell."

"Miss Abcott? Miss Mildred from the front desk said you registered the room under the name of Mr. and Mrs. Caleb Matthews." The priest did not back down.

"And if I did, what is it to you? As far as I can tell, it's none of your damned business!"

"Don't say da…that word," Danny begged.

"It's my business, because this young lady came to me seeking counsel. She explained what happened here last night and her fear ye might not do right by her." Father McKnight was shorter than the deputy and a good fifty pounds lighter. The fact that he appeared less than thirty-years-old might give most men pause concerning standing toe-to-toe with Caleb Matthews. But where innocent souls were at stake, the priest threw caution to the wind.

"Now *you* are going to start pressuring me into marrying her, too?" Caleb appeared dazed. "Damn, how far do I have to travel from Golden River before people stop demanding I give up my freedom?" Groaning, he sat on the bed, pulling Danny to sit beside him. Facing her, he finally spoke. "I will always do right by you, Daniella. Last night is a blur, right now. Let's go down and get something to eat, so we can discuss this like rational adults."

"I see blood on the bed sheet behind ye, sir." The priest crossed his arms. "It takes little imagination to surmise what happened here last night, even for a celibate man of the cloth, like meself."

Caleb turned to stare at the red spot on the bed. Daniella's blood. His own bloodshot eyes jerked up to Danny's face next. "It *wasn't* a dream? You and I…you let me… Damn it to hell, Danny, tell me you had the good sense to put a stop to things, last night. Lord knows, *I* was in no condition to make the right decisions."

"So yer going to lay all the blame on the lass' lap, eh? After she spoke so fondly of ye and all." He paused.

"But he *is* a man I can love and respect, Father," Daniella interrupted.

"Well," he commanded. "Prove the lass wasn't wrong. Show up at the chapel down the way in half an hour. I'll have everything ready to right this wrong. Ye'll have to say you are willing to learn the ways of the faith, son, and vow to raise yer children in the Catholic church."

"Stop rushing me," Caleb snapped. "I need time to think. Daniella and I will decide when and if we want you to marry us."

"Miss Abcott, I will not leave ye in this room, alone with a man who is not yer husband and has already shown his lack of better judgement." Father McKnight walked to the door and beckoned her to follow him. "Ye asked me to help get this man to the altar, lass. Come with me now. If it is truly meant to be, he will come of his own free will. If not, I'll help ye make decisions about the future and any child which might come from this ill-fated union."

"Children?" Caleb's voice was strained.

Danny couldn't stand the despair so plainly written on Caleb's face. With a muffled sob, she got up and followed the priest out of the room, praying silently that Caleb would come. He loved her, she promised herself. He would show up and take her as his wife.

AGONIZING...

Caleb sat there for a good five minutes, staring at the door that had closed with such finality. What had just happened? All he could hear was the last sob she had uttered before the priest dragged her out of the room. It would kill him, that sob.

He tried hard to remember what had happened the night before. Had Danny truly encouraged him to take her, or was that a figment of his imagination? Once again, he turned, looking down at the bed where the tell-tale red stain existed.

The priest was right. If he'd been tempted to ignore all that the man had said, standing in the doorway, this proved it.

Had Danny tricked him into marriage? Had she really believed he meant her to follow him to Sacramento to marry her? He would never have done that. If he'd intended to marry her, he'd have done it there, in Golden River, with Noah performing the ceremony. If he'd brought her to Sacramento, he'd have driven the wagon, himself, and made sure they both got there safely.

Leaning forward, he braced his elbows on his knees and leaned his head into his hands.

This was his own fault. All of it. He should have made sure Danny understood what his intentions were before he left town.

His head pounded as if someone had whacked him with an iron skillet.

Time was wasting. He could picture Daniella sitting in the chapel crying, wondering if she might be left to raise a baby—a baby of *his*—on her own. Or worse—give it to someone else to raise.

He couldn't stand it.

He stood, swaying, and waited until the room stopped moving before he reached for his shirt. Where were his clothes? Had he left his things somewhere? The shirt he'd opened with such force last night had no buttons left on it, and he cursed, looking around. In the corner, he found a small trunk and pulled a wrinkled shirt from it to put on. His trousers, one of only two pairs he had after Daniella had stolen his on their first meeting, he tugged on.

He found a hairbrush belonging to Daniella lying on the chest, dragged it through his hair, and tossed it on the bed. Catching a glance of his own reflection as he moved toward the door, he cursed again. He looked as if he'd aged ten years.

And as he started for the stairs, he felt it, too.

∼

WEEPING...

Daniella sat silently, waiting. This was not at all what she'd envisioned for a wedding day, if, indeed, there was to be a wedding. She didn't get to wear the lovely, white dress she had created for her special day. She wondered if Caleb had fallen asleep again after she left with Father McKnight.

The town clock clanged, a single lonely sound in the distance, but she had no idea what time it was. Was Caleb coming? Father McKnight came from the back as she waited, glancing at her and then toward the back of the church sadly. He had frowned and turned away just as he heard the clatter of the door.

Daniella turned. Her groom had showed up, after all, a few minutes past the allotted time set by the priest, and she tried to ignore his wrinkled shirt. His trousers, she recognized as the ones he'd worn yesterday. This was not the beautiful, perfect wedding she had dreamed of when she pictured becoming Caleb's wife.

The sacrament of matrimony was a blur. They signed the license in silence. The priest raised his hand to shake the groom's, and for a second, Danny feared Caleb would refuse. In the end, he grasped the hand and passed the man a few dollars to pay for his services. "Sorry we took up so much of your time, Father. You can rest assured, I will continue to do my duty by Daniella."

Then he walked out of the chapel, leaving Danny to follow behind him.

She watched him go, covering her face with her hands to hide her tears. "I should have known a man like Caleb wouldn't want me for his bride. He is miserable. I can see it clearly now." She couldn't raise her eyes. "He hates me. I know it."

"Do you love *him*, lass?" Father asked softly.

She nodded, hiccupping. "More than anyone in this world, Father. Or anything."

"Gettin' a man to wed ye is the easy part, then. Go fight to make the marriage work. Show him how lucky he is to have ye."

Danny waited, sure she could never face Caleb Matthews.

Where had he gone? Would he leave, never wanting to lay eyes on her again? She leaned against the wall, weeping tears of grief, and eventually slid to the floor and wrapped her arms around her knees, continuing to weep for what seemed like hours. When she opened her eyes, Father McKnight had disappeared, and she was alone.

She decided there was no other choice open to her. They were married in the eyes of the Lord, now. Surely, Caleb had feelings for her. Last night could not have been solely the result of a drunken haze. When they made love, it had been beautiful, magical. At least, they had that going for them. In time, Caleb would find it easier to accept her as his wife. Until then, she would work hard, be on her best behavior, and give him nothing but good things to say about her.

Forcing a smile on her face, she pushed the tears away with the back of her hands and left the church, preparing to run all the way back to the hotel, if necessary, to catch up with her new husband.

She gasped as she stepped out the front door. Caleb was waiting just outside the chapel. She gulped, raising tear-stained eyes to his.

Caleb said nothing but turned toward the hotel, holding out an arm for her to take. Once she was beside him, they walked slowly, side by side, back to their room. Not a single word was spoken.

But once the door was closed, things changed. "Congratulations, my girl. You outwitted me yet again." He leaned against the doorframe and studied her.

Her expression sad and full of guilt, she whispered, "I have never outwitted you, Caleb."

He continued on as if she had not spoken. "First, you stole my clothes, leaving me bare-assed in the sun, stranded in broad daylight. But this time, I feel even more exposed. Wait until it gets out that a sheriff's deputy was tricked into marriage by a tiny, half pint of a girl."

"Tricked you!" Danny forgot all about her promise to be a perfect wife. "It was your idea to come to Sacramento to get married, remember?"

"It was my idea to come here to avoid getting married!" he roared back.

Her chest heaved with frustration. She walked to the side of the bed and picked up a water pitcher. For a moment, she stood there, holding it. "You talked about marrying me. You winked in my direction and said you were leaving town. Then you kissed me and asked if I understood your meaning. What was I *supposed* to think?" Taking careful aim, she hurled it with all her might at his head. The pitcher fell, well-short of its target, because as mad as she was, she didn't have the heart to really case him injury. He simply leaned forward and caught it, setting it down.

"I talked about marrying you on my own terms. I said I was leaving town to put some distance between us. I was giving you a good-bye kiss!"

Danny's eyes widened, and Caleb held up his hand as if to calm her down, but she was angry enough now to spit.

"You were going to leave me behind? You bastard!" The bowl, which matched the pitcher she threw, made contact, albeit a passing graze on his right shoulder as he dodged the whole impact, grabbing it. "So, Tobias was *lying* when he said you were planning on coming to the ranch to see me before you left town." She started laughing, but it was not a joyful sound. It was full of embarrassment, bitterness, and regret. "Why did you register this room as if we were married if you never planned for me to show up here?"

"I didn't have much chance now, did I? You tricked poor Henry into bringing you here and ordered him to head back home, so I would have no choice but to take responsibility for you. Stupid me, I thought to protect your honor by renting a room for you to stay in until I could bring your bratty backside back to Golden River." He raised his hands to protect his face. "Hang that damn lantern back on the wall, Daniella. If you toss it at me, so help me, I'll tan your backside black and blue."

"So, while I was waiting up here, expecting you to show up with someone to marry us, you were off at the bar, drinking yourself into a stupor so you could try to forget I even existed? Tell me, who else did you take to your bed while you were there?" Rage began to seethe in her veins. This time, she chose the large green vase that sat on the side of the bed and picked it up with both hands. But instead of aiming for his head, she launched it at his groin.

For once in her life, she was too fast for him. Caleb caught it but too late. White-faced, he dropped to his knees, his hands reaching to cover his injured section. His eyes rolled back for a moment, and Danny immediately regretted her action and rushed to kneel beside him.

"Oh, Caleb! I'm so sorry!"

He didn't speak for several moments, but the expression on his white face reflected that of a wounded animal. Slowly, eventually, he rose to his feet. Cursing herself for not remembering how dangerous wounded animals were, Danny tried to move out of reach.

It was too late.

He was on his feet, lifting her and carting her toward the bed. Once there, he plopped down and forced her over his legs, baring her bottom. His hand began pounding, gaining more force with each contact. "Stealing my clothes and freedom wasn't enough for you? Now, you want to render me unfit for fatherhood, too?" He stopped a moment and reached for the hairbrush he'd thrown down on the bed, earlier, using that to pepper her bottom with extremely hard swats.

His arm appeared to tire out long before his frustration. "This is not finished, Danny girl. I am going to walk away before I do or say something we will both regret. I expect you to stay here and think about changing your ways. We may be married now, but I will not put up with a woman who undermines me at every turn."

He pulled her upright and sat her down, hard, into the nearby chair. He meant the impact to sting, and it did. Danny, however, refused to give him the satisfaction of yelping. "Tell me, Caleb. Were you ever going to lower your standards and marry plain old Daniella Abcott?" she demanded before he walked out the door.

Caleb considered his answer. Stopping just inside, he turned to face her. "There is nothing plain about you, Daniella Matthews. The sooner you see that, the better off you'll be, and the faster you'll grow up. Then, perhaps you'll stop trying to be something you're not and realize what a beautiful woman you are. I expect you to become as beautiful on the inside as you are on the outside." He stared at her for a long moment before continuing. "And the answer is no. Not on this trip, that's for sure. And certainly, not by a cranky old priest with a condemning voice and a funny accent. Like it or not, Daniella Matthews, you need to understand I came here to put off the pressure of getting married. Lot of good it did me." He glared at her a moment longer before continuing. "Stay put, young lady. This discussion is far from over."

She ran to lock the door behind him before bursting into tears. What a fool she had been! "I'll go back east," she sobbed toward the door. "At least, there, people love me." But she did not have enough funds to make the journey home yet. She'd have to find a way to make some money. Caleb would no doubt try to track her down and bring her back. Now that they were married, he would feel honor-bound to do so. "Don't worry, I'm going to give you your freedom back, Caleb Matthews." She saw the marriage license the priest had given him lying on the floor. His vows to her were left where they could be walked on.

Or destroyed, as her life was, this very moment.

# CHAPTER 6

*C*aleb stood outside the door a long time, trying to decide whether or not to go back in. He closed his eyes, listening to her miserable sobbing. Wishing he hadn't spanked her as hard as he did, he hung his head, hating himself for being so hard on her.

Slowly, he moved toward the steps and quietly descended them, one at a time, trying to make up his mind whether to keep going or go back.

He kept going, his troubled thoughts giving him no rest. Glad there was no one at the desk, he exited the door and turned right. He passed the chapel but didn't go in. What had made Danny go and seek a priest's council? He knew she was in search of someone to marry them, but was it because she'd seen the red stain? Why didn't she awaken him? She could trust him enough to be her husband but not enough to make decisions?

He'd have done the right thing. He wished she'd known that.

He wondered if she was pregnant. There was no way he would allow her to have his child and raise it by herself. Nor was there any way he'd allow her to give up their child. He needed to let her know that. Despite his flaws, and there were a multitude of them, he was determined to be a good husband, a good father. It was sooner than he expected, that was all. He loved her. He adored her. He knew it.

He turned back toward the hotel.
She needed to know it, too.

~

He'd gotten further than he realized from the hotel, when he turned back, and added speed to his steps. He'd sit with her in his lap and try to console her. This was his responsibility, after all, and he intended to fulfill it. He hoped she didn't hate him too much. But one thing he would not have was Daniella hurling heavy objects at his groin. It was unthinkable.

Nodding at the woman behind the desk who gave him an uncertain glance, he hurried up the steps to the third floor and down the hall. Automatically, he put a hand on the doorknob and turned, reaching into his pocket for the key.

The door moved inward, and Caleb paused abruptly, realizing it was unlocked. He stood there, staring at the room. Daniella was nowhere to be seen.

"Daniella?" He stepped forward, away from the door, glancing behind it to see if she was hiding there.

The bed was stripped of linen. It was piled in the basket in the corner of the room. The lamps had been blown out, and the pitcher and bowl he'd rescued in her attempts to throw them at him were set back in the washstand. Her trunks had been pushed into the corner, but there was something odd about them. Daniella was so small; he didn't understand how she could have moved them. Had someone else?

He moved toward them. The key was in the lock? Opening the lock on the one nearest him carefully, he stared at it. Her wedding dress was tucked neatly inside, along with a sheer lacy garment that resembled a night dress. Frowning, he pulled it out.

A piece of parchment fluttered to the floor, and he reached for it.

"*Daniella?*" Quickly, he moved to the window as the breeze caused the curtains to flutter. From up here, he could see several blocks down the street. That's why she'd seen him last night when he came out of the saloon.

He held up the paper and read.

*Dearest Caleb,*

*May I call you that one last time? I promise never to again. I knew you didn't want me from the beginning.*

*I'm sorry I've ruined your life. You left the marriage license behind, so I assumed you didn't want it. I left it for you, on the bed. You may do whatever you want—even destroy it. It would seem appropriate, since I've destroyed your life. I almost threw it in the fire, but the way things ordinarily happen for me, I feared burning down the hotel.*

*No one knows about our marriage except Father McKnight, so do with it whatever you want. If, however, you want to pursue it further, he can have the ceremony annulled for you. I understand.*

*Once more, Caleb, I'm so sorry.*

*Daniella Abcott*

Caleb stared at the letter in his hand, stunned by the way she had signed her name. Abcott? She wasn't Daniella Abcott anymore; she was *Daniella Matthews.* He turned toward the bed, to see the marriage license she spoke of. It was torn in half, and both pieces were lying on the bare mattress, one piled on top of the other.

Damn!

He never should have left her alone.

"*Daniella?*" He knew he was alone, but there was still hope in his voice. It echoed back at him in the empty room.

Daniella was gone.

A WEEK LATER...

Rain pelted down on Danny as she slowly made her way back to Sacramento. Her dress was sticking to her, and she was shaking with cold. God must surely be mad at her. The last few days had been more horrible than any she had ever experienced. Her boots, as well as her reputation, were ruined. Mud seeped through the leather, and her feet were sore after three days of walking. Any chance she had of finding a decent job were truly lost now.

But the loss of a job wasn't what disturbed her. Caleb's stern face stayed constantly in front of her vision. She loved that face, but the disappointment in his eyes broke her heart. She couldn't bear having pushed him away so far that she'd never see a smile in his eyes again.

She wondered what he'd thought, when he went back to the hotel and found her note and the wedding license ripped up on top of the bed. Had he found her note and read it? Had he even seen it? Perhaps he'd tossed it all into the fireplace without even looking at it.

The truth was he didn't want her. The feeling of rejection tore at her heart as tears crept down her cheeks. She'd even had trouble asking people for work without crying. She knew her eyes were red. It must have lowered her chances for being hired. No one wanted to hire a weeping woman full of need.

Having to walk everywhere on foot limited her choices, too. She'd tried to stay within a few miles walking distance from town. She'd tried for work at every place she passed, since leaving the hotel a few days before. Most people had offered her a meal and encouraged her to go home. Some had given her an idea where she might go next. She'd asked for work at a ranch outside Sacramento, a few miles away. The cook had come to the door and invited her in, feeding her a meal before sending her away. She'd walked back to town, weary and exhausted.

Next, Danny had tried to hire on at the saloon. The woman in the kitchen offered her food, too, but said there were no positions available.

"Sit down, child, and rest your feet while you eat," the woman had urged. "Your boots are about to fall off your feet." She'd turned away to pull a large plate from a stack and filled it with beans and cornbread. It smelled delicious.

She set it down in front of Danny. "You ran away from home,

didn't you?" When she saw the disappointed expression on Daniella's face, she continued. "It's a foolish decision. child. I know firsthand. My papa wouldn't let me wed the beau I wanted and I took off in a pique of fury. Look around you, girl. This is your future if you don't heed my warning. I ended up having to marry a barkeep and work all hours of the night and day. It never ends. The girls in front at least get some rest; we see to that. But they work as hard as I do, and we don't need any more right now."

Danny was embarrassed at the way she nearly inhaled the food on her plate. "Thank you, ma'am, for the meal. Are you sure there isn't something I can do to repay you? I mean, I haven't any money right now, but..."

A sympathetic smile took away some of the woman's severity. She took Danny's empty dinner plate and replaced it with a slice of apple pie. "Course, it could have been worse. My Jimmy is a good, God-fearing man. If it hadn't been for him, I might have ended up working at the brothel tucked near the far corner of the town."

Hope and dread both took hold of Danny's heart. Was she desperate enough to try for honest work there? Looking down at her bare feet, she had her answer. They were reddened from the roughness of the boots that were coming apart in places. Pink toes were exposed through the side, and she didn't have the money to replace them.

"Stay here a moment, child," the woman said, disappearing toward the door to the saloon.

Danny nodded as she left. *A brothel?* She'd heard of those. She wondered if there was any place there to work that didn't include bedding strange men. She had no desire to work as a call girl. For better or worse, she had made a promise to love, honor, and obey Caleb. Her brows knit together in a scowl. Obey him? She certainly hadn't done very well at that. While she'd freed him from their vows, she would never dishonor him.

She glanced up when the woman returned. In her hands, she had a pair of old boots and some stockings.

"The girls upstairs sent these down for you. The boots are well-used, but they're better than what you're wearing. See if they fit. You can't keep walking in the ones you have. They'll ruin your feet. Wait." She turned away for a moment and brought a pail of something into view. "Drink this. It won't keep you forever, but you need nourishment."

Daniella looked down into the cup the woman handed her. It was full of cool milk, and her eyes became misty. Wrapping her hands around the mug, she sipped. When she was able to set it down, she gulped, touched by the woman's kindness.

"Thank you, ma'am," she whispered, "for being so kind. And please thank the ladies who sent these down."

A nod answered her. The woman said nothing more, until Danny moved toward the back door.

A hand suddenly rested on her shoulder, and she looked up to see the woman's face, close. "If you go to the brothel," she said in little more than a whisper, "tell Lydia to try to find you a decent place, where you'll be safe. Tell her Sophie sent you."

"Yes, ma'am," she answered. "I'll do that."

## CHAPTER 7

SEARCHING...

Caleb fought the pounding of his head as he once again ended the day with no sign of his little wife. The pieces of the marriage certificate, he had carefully folded up and carried in his pocket. He'd pulled it out frequently and studied it, almost seeing the tiny hand and delicate fingers of Daniella as she'd signed. There had been some trembling there, too, in that signature.

Dear God. How could he have been such a bastard? Even if he found her, she would probably never speak to him again. He passed the saloon as he approached the hotel once again and considered going inside for a drink but decided against it.

The trip up the steps was long as he dragged one foot up after another. He'd looked everywhere he possibly could. There was no sign of her. Once, he thought he'd found a woman who had seen her. A young girl had come in, asking for work, but the woman had nothing to offer her, and she'd gone on her way.

"I'm sorry, sir. Has she run away?"

He gulped. Indeed, she had, but he couldn't bring himself to admit she'd run from him. It broke his heart to think she'd tried to find work, to survive.

The next person who had seen her was the barkeep in the saloon.

"Talk to my wife," he said, motioning toward the kitchen.

A pretty woman stood over the stove, stirring a pot. When he stood in the doorway, she glanced up.

"Your husband sent me," he croaked out. "I'm looking for a young lady, tiny, brown hair, brown eyes. She might have been looking for work."

She dropped the spoon in a plate beside the pot and turned to him. "There was a girl here recently. Pretty little thing. Truth is we could have used another girl in the front, but she didn't look the type. She looked like a scared little girl. I felt sorry for her, and I did feed her before she left. But she looked too young, too innocent, to work here." She put her hands, in fists, on her hips, and faced him. "My question to you, young man, is why was she running from you?"

Caleb stared back. "Have you any idea where she went?"

"None," she said. "And I'm not sure I'd tell you if I did. But if she's afraid of you, there's a reason."

Caleb's mouth was tight, and he turned back toward the saloon, making his way through the crowd and out the swinging doors. He stood there in the street, running his fingers through his hair, angry —not at her but at himself.

What she'd said was absolutely true. Daniella was young, vulnerable, and he was responsible for her, for her welfare, for her happiness. And he'd failed her.

Miserably.

~

Sitting on a log a few doors down from the saloon, Daniella glanced up and jumped to her feet, moving around the side of the building to keep from being seen. None other than Caleb, with his hands jammed into his pockets, had caught her eye. His shoulders sagged, and he appeared exhausted. More than that, he looked extremely sad. Something was sticking up out of his shirt pocket. She gasped. Was it the marriage certificate?

Her first instinct was to run to him and beg him to forgive her. Unsure what kept her from it, she stood there, frozen, her eyes wide. His face was gaunt; he looked as if he hadn't taken the time to eat for days. She wondered if he needed money, too. Unable to take her eyes off those strong, masculine shoulders, she watched as he dragged himself toward the hotel. Her heart sank. She'd not only ruined her own life, she'd ruined his.

Thus far, she had begged for work, seeking whatever tasks might be available. Maybe it was time to change techniques. Danny would start listing the various tasks she was skilled to take on. "I am a seamstress, a fair cook, an excellent maid…"

With Caleb out of sight now, she stood up to move toward the brothel, repeating those qualities, again and again. Her concentration was so intense, she didn't realize she had walked straight into the path of a wagon. The driver managed to yank back on the reins just in time as the horses reared. Daniella jerked her head upward and threw up her hands, apologizing.

But within minutes, a man hurriedly carrying a tray of food toward the jail was forced to stop; she was inches before him. "Look out!" he shouted, trying to right himself. But it was too late. His balance compromised by the heavy tray, he ended up traveling several feet sideways, the food on the tray ending up on his clothes.

"Whoa! Watch where you're going, girlie!" he yelled angrily

Daniella met the eyes of an angry man. "Oh! I'm sorry, sir!" The apology in her voice was genuine as she stepped back.

"You should be. There were a bunch of hungry prisoners waiting on this."

Her first thought was to offer to pay for the food, but there was no point. She had nothing to pay with. Backing away, she moved down the street as he disappeared back in the direction he had come.

Daniella allowed a heavy sigh to escape and continued moving toward the end of the street. But when a shrill whistle from the second floor of a colorful building caused her to lose her concentration completely, she blinked. Head thrown back, she looked upward toward the sound. A pretty woman with long, tousled hair hung out of an open window. Danny gasped when she realized the woman's chemise was sliding down one shoulder, exposing most of her voluptuous breasts.

She started to call out a warning toward the window above, just as a tall man came from the back of the house, walking toward her. He stopped to turn in the same direction. But before Danny could utter a word, the woman laughed toward him.

"Sheriff, you forgot your badge."

The man standing directly in front of Daniella raised his hands wildly in an attempt to quiet the naked woman down. He rushed back toward the brothel and motioned for her to throw him the forgotten item.

"Don't I get a reward for returning it?" she pouted, leaning further out of the window.

"I don't have time for your nonsense, Leanna. My wife will be expecting me for dinner. Toss it to me, so I can be on my way." The man tried to keep his voice calm, but Daniella saw the anger in his reddened face.

She was beginning to feel as if she should step back from the scene, when another woman walked around the side of the building. Older and quite large, she glanced first at the sheriff, then upward toward the window. The woman called Leanna leaned back inside the window as she saw her approach.

Daniella gave a startled jump as the old lady opened her mouth. Her sympathetic face and her croaky voice didn't seem to match at all.

"Give the man his property."

Leanna barely inched her face out of the window this time.

"Don't go getting upset, Miss Berthie. I was getting ready to give it back. It's not my fault he left it behind."

"He left it behind?" The old woman frowned. "More than likely, you swiped it when he wasn't looking. Give it back."

The sheriff caught the flash of silver as it flew in his direction. Pinning it back on his shirt, he nodded his appreciation toward the woman named Berthie. "That one may have an angel's face, but she has a devil's sense of mischief. I warned Madam Lydia before she hired her."

The old woman glared back up at him. "Yet you choose to bed her?"

"Well." He looked uncomfortable as he eyed Daniella, who stood curiously before him. "She does a few things the other girls won't even consider. While my dear wife is ill, she encouraged me to seek relief here."

Berthie put her shoulders back and glared at him. "Sheriff, if you want to lie to yourself about being faithful to your wife, I won't judge you. But don't act all self-righteous about our girls. You best be heading home to your wife. I need to finish tending to my garden before nightfall."

Danny tried to pretend she was wasn't listening, but her mouth hung open a moment or two as the sheriff huffed away.

"Down on your luck, eh?" The old woman stepped toward her. Danny nodded silently, trying to remember the words she had practiced all the way over here. No coherent words formed. At last, she gulped and forced out, "Sophie sent me, ma'am."

Berthie eyed her, shaking her head. "I swear, you girls get younger and younger. Well, close your mouth and follow me. You can tell me about your circumstances while you help me haul in my vegetables." Berthie's large feet made wide prints in the mud as she walked back toward the side of the building. Danny stepped inside them, following cautiously.

She found her voice suddenly. "I'm not as young as you might think, ma'am. And I'm much more skilled than I appear. I'm a seamstress, a fair cook, an excellent maid…"

"You capable of lifting heavy baskets?" the woman demanded. Daniella smiled and nodded her head as Berthie stopped and pointed to a large woven basket filled with vegetables. "Show me."

The basket was heavier than it looked and required bending down deep to get a solid grip on the handles, but she managed. Slowly, she carried the load toward a side door Berthie indicated. On the way, Berthie riddled her with questions. Her name? Where was she from? What kind of experience did she have? Daniella tried her best to answer them with confidence.

Never having been inside a brothel before, Daniella was unsure what she expected to find there. She looked around, slightly disappointed. The kitchen was plain and much like the kitchen at the ranch. A pang of homesickness hit, and she looked away, wondering if they missed her.

"Set it down over there," Berthie croaked, nodding toward the table, "and put them in the sink to wash. And put this on." She tossed Daniella an apron. "I'll go and get the madam." She left the room and closed the door behind her as Danny began tying the apron around her waist.

Daniella looked wildly about her. What was she doing? Alone in the kitchen, she turned toward the door. She still had a chance to run, but where else was there to go? She had tried everywhere, with no success at all. But even as the thought occurred, she heard footsteps returning. Quickly, she began placing the vegetables onto the apron and carrying them across to the sink.

The door flew open, and she gasped, unsure what to expect. Berthie stepped inside and made room for another woman, a beautiful one, at that. She stood there quietly as Daniella helped sort out the basket's contents to wash.

The voice of this woman was as beautiful as her face. "Berthie, have you found another stray kitten? This one looks a bit young, as if she's yet to be weaned."

"Sophie sent this one," Berthie announced. "Daniella Abcott, meet Madam Lydia," the old woman announced. "Go on, girlie. Tell her about all your fancy skills."

Madam Lydia was breathtakingly beautiful. Red curls hung around her oval face. Though light, her lashes were thick and drew attention to her emerald eyes.

Daniella, who already felt plain, was ashamed of her unkempt condition. "I-I…"

Berthie chuckled and tapped her on the shoulder. "The girl's a seamstress."

"Did you make the dress you're wearing?" A smile lit Lydia's face.

Glancing down at her soiled dress, Danny's face grew crimson. The lower foot of material was stained with mud. It looked old and tattered compared to the garments Lydia wore. Danny gulped loudly. "Yes, ma'am, but it used to be in much better condition."

The madam nodded kindly. "Perhaps, but I can see the fine quality of your stitching. Besides sewing, do you have any other talents?"

Daniella realized the woman was not mocking her but seemed truly interested in hearing about her skills. "Well, I…"

"She's a fair cook," Berthie declared as she started washing the things collected from the garden.

The emerald-eyed Lydia pulled out a seat and lowered herself into it. "Can you help prepare and serve meals to feed several people? Our table welcomes as many as ten, at times. We could provide you material to make garments to wear. And you wouldn't be required to do all the cooking. Berthie is careful who she lets near her stove."

Daniella nodded, but no words left her lips. Berthie shook her head with frustration. "She helped cook at a ranch near Golden River for the last few months. But I wouldn't leave her alone at *my* stove." She paused a moment. "At least, she's not mouthy like the last girl we took in."

Lydia glanced toward Berthie then back at Daniella. Pulling out a chair, she patted the seat. "Rest your feet, Daniella, and take a few moments to gather your courage. I don't know what brought you here, but it's obvious to me, you need help." Lydia's voice was soft, almost musical. "You don't have to worry. No one will judge you here."

She was unsure if it was the normal atmosphere or the kind eyes of both women, but eventually, Daniella felt comfortable enough to speak. "It's hard to explain my circumstances. I guess it all started when I agreed to travel out west as a mail order bride. The men in Golden River pooled their funds to help pay for my passage. In return, it was understood I would have my pick of the available men to wed."

At the mention of being a mail order bride, Madam Lydia seemed to stiffen, but Daniella concluded she must have imagined it because, soon, the other woman was nodding and encouraging her to continue with her tale. "My new friends, Obie and Jeddah, along with myself, ended up staying at a ranch outside of Golden River because there was no hotel in town at the time."

"And did you find a man in town to your liking?" Madam Lydia asked, pushing over a steaming cup of tea.

"Yes, ma'am, I did. And my life is a mess now because of it. I fell in love with the perfect man. He is everything a woman could want in a husband. He's handsome, of course, but it's his personality which defines him. Caleb, that's his name, protects the weak. He has a strong sense of right and wrong and a heart as pure as gold."

Berthie sat beside Daniella and patted her shoulder. "He didn't return your affections?" she asked.

Danny blushed, recalling all the times she spent with Caleb, realizing the signs were there from the very start. "He distanced himself from me every chance he got. But on rare occasions," she sighed, "he acted as if he returned my feelings. There were stolen kisses and sweet words. It was hard to reconcile, but every time I lost heart, my friend, Jeddah, would convince me Caleb was smitten with me, too. More brides started arriving in town, and I was sure he would fall for a prettier lady who was more refined. I guess that's when the real trouble started."

"Go on," Madam Lydia encouraged.

"I rushed him to be married," Danny managed to admit. "I

convinced myself the entire thing was his idea, misreading every sign he gave me. He left town to escape me, but I thought he wanted me to join him here, so we could get married."

"Did you hold a gun to his head during the wedding ceremony?" Berthie mocked.

"Worse." Danny slumped in her seat, the weight of guilt overwhelming her. "I had a priest shame him into marrying me. Caleb had rented a room at the hotel under both our names. When he came to bed drunk, the first night here, we…we…" Even though she was talking to women who ran a brothel, Daniella couldn't bring herself to admit her lapse in morals.

"You made love," Lydia finished for her.

Berthie nodded. "Child, stop beating up on yourself."

A smile from Lydia was comforting. 'You love the man, and it's only natural to fall victim to passions when you are far from prying eyes. So, Caleb married you, which proves he is a decent man, like you said. I don't see where the trouble is, Daniella."

"After the marriage, he was bluntly honest about his resentment toward me and my actions. In his eyes, I *tricked* him into marriage. He believes I schemed and did everything in my power to force him into something he wasn't ready for. We had a horrible fight, and he stormed out. Any hopes of having a happy marriage were gone."

Madam Lydia folded her hands together as she regarded Danny. "You ran away and ended up here. There is still time to fix things. If you go back now, the two of you could work things out. Maybe he hasn't even returned to your hotel room yet."

"I left the hotel over a week ago," Danny admitted. "I've been trying to get a job so I can save enough funds to return home. I have family there. I'd rather not go back to Golden River. I know everyone there will laugh at me."

"But if your husband is looking for you?" Lydia asked softly.

"It would be out of responsibility, instead of love. I've lost everything, including my pride. If I find myself with his child, I'll go back, because it would be wrong to deny Caleb a role in his child's life. But, God willing, my menses will start in a few weeks and I can continue with my plans to go back east."

Lydia nodded and took in her words before speaking again. "Daniella, you can stay here until you discover which path your future holds. Berthie can use the help. I have only one rule you must agree to follow."

"Anything," Danny agreed quickly.

"You must not go upstairs, for any reason. I'll see you get a bedroom downstairs. I know you aren't a virgin now, but even I am shocked by some of the things I have witnessed up there. After ten years, that is saying more than I want to admit." She frowned, a crease forming at the bridge of her nose. "Now, suppose your husband shows up here? Will you face him? I need to know, so we can prepare for any possible trouble."

"I prefer not to see him again until I know if I am carrying his baby."

"Berthie, do you have any suggestions about helping our new guest avoid confrontation?" Madam Lydia asked.

"How do you feel about wearing trousers?" the old woman demanded. "Before you go belly aching, you should know that moving around in men's clothes ain't nearly as complicated as dressing like a woman."

"I used to own my very own pair of pants and a nice shirt," Danny admitted. She had left them behind at the ranch because Caleb hated them. Partly, it was because she had stolen his own clothes to make them, but she knew the clothes reminded him of her impulsive nature.

"Well, then." Madam Lydia stood up and put out a hand. "Welcome, *Daniel.*" She smiled. "It seems you have a new job—*and* a new identity."

# CHAPTER 8

DECEPTION...

*J*eddah pushed her eggs around on her plate and ignored the chatter of the ranch hands around her at the table. Danny's chair was empty, as was Caleb's, yet it was another vacant place which terrified her this morning. Noah had not spent the night at the ranch, as had been his habit since her arrival. She had grown accustomed to having him nearby, inhaling his clean scent and listening to his calming tone. Now, thanks to her habit of boasting, she might never share a meal with the man who had captured her heart, all those months before.

It had all started off so harmlessly, she pondered—a little white lie meant to comfort her parents back home. Shaking her head, Jeddah realized that was not true. She wanted to brag and rub her good fortune in the faces of all those people back in her hometown, the ones who claimed she would never amount to much. She had penned a letter to her mother, knowing word would spread. Mama never could keep a secret, and Jeddah was taking advantage of it. She had spoken of finding the love of her life, a man everyone in town looked up to and respected.

It was true, though worded vaguely to imply Noah was wealthy and powerful, all the things she swore she would find when she traveled out west to find a husband. Biting her lip, she tried to justify her bragging. What he lacked in money, Noah more than made up for in spirit, character, and determination. He worked his small farm and saw to the religious needs of his community. And everyone did look up to him.

People around town had the utmost respect for Noah. Attendance at the small church he ran had doubled since women had arrived in town. A frown marred Jeddah's lip. Even the new brides were regular worshipers now, and because of it, so were the men. She still remembered seeing Hester sitting in the center of the front row at the Sunday service. The quiet brunette had met Jeddah's eye with no indication of their past relationship.

Hester was biding her time, Jeddah decided, waiting to tell everyone what a sinful, lying woman the preacher had begun seeing. Still, it did not matter what everyone in town thought. Jeddah only cared about one person's reaction. Would Noah be angry about her bragging? Or would he be embarrassed by feeling the need to build him up into something he wasn't?

"Come on, girl. Out with it," Faith said, startling her out of her moping.

She glanced up, surprised to see Faith staring at her from a few places away at the table. Everyone else had departed without her even noticing. Swallowing hard, Jeddah wished again that Danny was here. Though they had their share of spats, it was nice to have someone to confide in. She could not even try discussing this matter with Obie. Tobias rarely left his new bride's side. Besides, Obie spent more time losing the contents of her stomach than chatting, these days.

"You aren't fretting about Danny's disappearance, are you? Caleb's watching out for her. I trust him to keep her safe, and you should, too." Though much older, Faith was a new blushing bride, herself.

Jeddah frowned. In spite of the weddings that had taken place since she arrived, she and Daniella still remained unwed. *Well, perhaps not.* Danny was no doubt married now, too. That left only Jeddah.

"Jeddah?" Faith's voice was concerned.

"I'll be the last of the brides to make it to the altar," she moaned. "I bet every last one of the new mail order brides finds a husband before I do."

"Nonsense. Noah has as good as put a ring on your finger, child. He's a man of God. He wouldn't court you just to set you aside and take up with a new woman." Faith patted Jeddah's back as the younger girl choked out a tiny sob.

"But I'm not worthy of a decent man like Noah. I knew it was only a matter of time before he realized that, but I admit, I had hoped we would be good and married a few years before it occurred to him. My past is coming back to haunt me, Aunt Faith. One of the new brides from back east, the one who sat next to you in Sunday services, is from my hometown."

"Why does her presence worry you?" Faith prompted.

"Everyone back there knows what a selfish, proud fool I used to be. Oh, Faith, before I left home, I practically stood in the center of town and told everyone I was moving away because I was so much better than the lot of them. Hester was one of the people who heard my horrible declaration. She didn't laugh in my face, but she gave me a strange stare. I'm sure she was thinking what an absolute idiot I was."

"More than likely, she was thinking you were brave to strike out on your own. It took a lot of courage to leave home and seek a better future out here. She did follow your example, after all. As for your past ways, you have matured a lot since coming here. I've seen it." A chuckle escaped, and Faith's eyes twinkled. "I'd like to think it's because of my influence, but we both know it's not. The honor belongs to a special, young man who has claimed your affections. He fell in love with the woman you've become, not the child who arrived."

Jeddah rushed to tell it all, before she lost her nerve. "Well, I must still have some growing up to do, because I did something so awful, Noah will never want to set eyes on me again. I hope to goodness he doesn't find out—"

She froze as the screen door clanged shut, just as a deep voice spoke sternly, echoing around the room. "Trust me, I do want to set eyes on you, young lady. It will make tanning your backside easier."

Jeddah didn't need to turn her head to recognize the deep, commanding voice of the new arrival. She sank deeper in her seat, begging Faith with her eyes not to abandon her.

But Faith's response was disappointing. She met Jeddah's eyes and shook her head. "I need to go hang some things on the line to dry." She pulled Jeddah's fingers free from her apron. "It's best to face him now. I don't know what you did, but I think you're about to learn never to do it again. I'll keep everyone clear of the house. It's the best I can offer." With one last pat of reassurance on the shoulder, she slipped out of the kitchen and closed the door.

Frozen in place, Jeddah waited for Noah's next move. The chair she sat on protested as it was pulled out and turned sideways. Her eyes slowly traveled up a worn shirt, a firm jaw that was pulsing, a flattened, grim mouth, and came to rest on glinting eyes that were narrowed down at her.

"I just had a long talk with your friend, Hester."

Jeddah's shoulders sagged. "She's hardly a friend," she offered. But she regretted opening her mouth as soon as she spoke. Noah's glare down at her was severe.

Noah yanked out another chair and turned it toward hers. Then he sat down and stared at her for a moment. Jeddah felt as if he was seeing every stain on her sinful soul for the first time. "Hester would be hurt to hear you say that. She spoke highly of you. You are her hero, the reason she mustered up the courage to leave her abusive father's home to come west."

"Abusive? I-I didn't know." A small ray of hope filled Jeddah's heart. Maybe Hester had not turned Noah against her, after all.

His next words snuffed out her optimism. "Hester is a shy young lady. She wanted to seek you out and ask to be introduced to your wealthy, powerful beau. She hopes the lucky man will be able to advise her on potential husbands."

"Shy? More like greedy. She probably wants to steal *my* man." The words escaped before she had a chance to stop them, and again, she regretted speaking.

Noah seemed even more upset with her, suddenly. "Are you ashamed of me, Jeddah? Is marrying a lowly farmer and preacher beneath you? Because if it is, say the word now, and I will step aside and let you set your sights on another man."

Jeddah popped out of her seat immediately. Dropping to her knees, she wrapped her arms around his leg and lay her head over on his thigh, trying to explain. "There is no other man for me, Noah. When I wrote that letter about finding a wealthy, powerful man, I…" She gulped. "I was still coming to terms with my true feelings for you. Back home, I always felt everyone looked down on me." She stopped and amended her explanation. "That's not true. I was the one who was judging others and feeling I was so much better than all of them, planning on coming out west to find a rich, powerful husband. Only, I found someone who was rich in a way money can't buy and powerful enough to make me want to be a better person, someone worthy of love."

Noah's gaze rested on her silently for what seemed an eternity before he spoke. "I do love you, Jeddah, but I need to know you love me for *who I am*, not who you *want* me to be. I'm not a rich man. Any power I have comes from serving the Lord. My wife will have to accept that. As for being a better person, I can promise I will love you enough to guide you back to the proper trail if you stray too far."

He loved her. Jeddah pushed away her tears and raised her chin, meeting his eyes. She hadn't lost him yet. Pulling herself up, she stood before him, ready to prove she was worth a second chance. "Please be patient with me, sir. So long as you are on the trail with me, I'll welcome your guidance. I can't stand the thought of losing you."

His mouth changed into an almost indulgent smile. "I'm glad to hear it." Noah reached upward, taking her face into his hands, and planted a deep kiss on her lips.

Jeddah sighed with relief, but only a second later, she gasped as he took her hand and pulled her so swiftly, she thought she would topple over. He saved her from hitting the floor, settling her across his hard lap. Her squeal of alarm went unnoticed as the echo of loud smacks rained down on her backside. "Lucky for you, sweetheart, I am an excellent trail master. You can count on me to drive home any lessons necessary." But his voice changed as he paused. "You aren't feeling a thing through this thick material, are you?"

Shrieking, Jeddah tried to free herself as she felt the hem of her dress being lifted. "Stop. Noah! Please. You, of all people, should know it's not decent to see me without—"

"Without covering?" He paused for a second, his hand resting on the small of her back. Then he whispered something which made her blush, "I may be a man of God, Jeddah, but my feelings for you remind me daily that I am only human. Seeing your delightful bottom, knowing I can only redden it instead of stroke it, is *my* penance. The thoughts I'm having right now are anything but pure. I might have to double the time I spend reddening it, but I'm determined you'll learn your lesson."

As he continued bringing his hard hand down over and over again, Jeddah thought about the guidance he was giving. She needed to grow up even more and thought about the changes she could make. He held her in his lap, when he finished, and whispered forgiveness into her ear softly. He echoed his earlier words of love but also promised he'd do this again if she didn't improve.

Jeddah found herself a changed woman after that morning. Sitting was a challenge, but she walked with pride. Noah loved her, sins and all. She decided to spend her life proving he chose well. When he sent her back upstairs to her room, she began to make plans. She'd take on extra chores and try to make up for the loss of Danny's help at the ranch. It was only after Faith insisted on paying her more for the added work that Jeddah came up with the plan to use the funds to improve the church.

She knew Noah would not accept her offer of money, so she would try to convince him to install an offering box in the back of the church. If the men were embarrassed at the small sums they could donate to the church, it would allow the people of Golden River to support their church without being ashamed of whatever amount they gave. But she wanted to become the most generous person to fill the little box. If she made enough doing her chores, she'd buy some material and make Noah a new pair of trousers. After that, she'd give enough money to replace the old rickety pulpit he preached from.

She reached into the wardrobe to see how much money she had left and sighed. The amount was dismally small but possibly enough to buy material to make him a new pair.

She loved Noah with all her heart. And she was determined to make him proud.

# CHAPTER 9

WORKING HARD...

Jeddah hesitated mid-step when she saw Hester sitting near the back of the church the following Sunday. Everyone else had left, mingling outside, discussing current happenings with each other. Noah was probably walking around, shaking hands, and offering advice when asked. The people of Golden River held the man she loved in high regard.

Her mind wandered as she glanced at Hester. If the girl had kept her mouth closed, no one would have known about the ridiculous letter, and sitting on the hard wooden pew would not have been so difficult this morning.

But she shook her head. It was too easy to blame others for her own misdeeds. Her lapse in judgement was not Hester's doing. It was her own. Jeddah was trying to keep from blaming others for her own errors, and Noah was trying to teach her that. Hester had not written the ill-fated, boastful comments which threatened her happiness with Noah. No, the sinful act had been her own foolish blunder. Thank goodness, Noah saw past the childish action, and they had worked through it.

The man she loved was so much wiser than most. He saw beyond the false face people tended to put on in public, He also found good, where other's failed to see it. Noah thought Hester was a decent person, one who survived a harsh background and longed to have a better future. Perhaps he was right. Maybe Jeddah had been wrong about her, all along.

She felt a bit ashamed at not knowing about Hester's tragic background. Her family back east had always appeared so normal, much like Jeddah's. The only difference in their families lay in the fact that Hester's seemed more patient and more loving.

Jeddah's shoulders drooped as she moved forward to find the broom and sweep away the dusty footprints always left in the sanctuary. Guilt made her resolved to forge a new friendship with her acquaintance. Which of the men in town might possibly make a good match for Hester?

"Jeddah Cromwell, I bet you never thought you would see someone from back home this far west."

Jeddah paused, turning. Hester was a few years younger, with large green eyes and dark hair which often drew attention. Jeddah had always seen her as a rival. How shallow her life had been before meeting Noah. "You must think me terribly rude, Hester. I've ignored you since you arrived."

A light chuckle followed. "I wasn't sure how you would react when you saw me. The entire journey west, I envisioned lots of different possibilities, from having me forcibly removed from town to welcoming me like a long-lost sister."

"Forcibly removed from town? Why would I?"

"According to your mother, you were marrying the most powerful man in Golden River," Hester said, a smile lighting her eyes.

Jeddah's face reddened. "My letter—I can't fathom why I did such a foolish thing. Back when I sent it, I was still clinging to resentment toward the people back home. I wanted to convince everyone I was better than any of them could hope to be. I'm surprised anyone believed a word of it."

"It was convincing," Hester assured her. "Oh, some people did laugh and say you were exaggerating, but I could see the jealousy in their eyes. I packed my bags and took every last bit of money I had stashed away under my mattress with me. I set out for Golden River within a week of your letter's arrival. Of course, I ran out of funds midway, but by then, an advertisement for more brides for Golden River reached the hotel where we stayed. Any doubts I had about your honesty were gone then. I was sure this area was plush with rich, successful men."

Jeddah had not considered her letter might cause such drastic measures. Had she lured poor Hester all this way because of her boastful lies? Her face filled with dismay. "Oh, dear."

"When we arrived at Golden River, I was sure there had been a terrible mistake. It wasn't possible this dried up old town could be the wonderful paradise you wrote about. Then I saw you at Sunday services, and slowly, I started to realize what happened."

"Oh, Hester, you must have wanted to kill me. I'm shocked you didn't call me out in front of everyone." She was glad Hester hadn't, however; it would likely have meant another spanking from Noah. "How can I make it up to you?"

"It'll be quite easy. I came to Golden River to find a husband and a better future."

*Didn't we all*, Jeddah thought. She turned and sat down in the pew only a few feet from Hester, with her back to the door. "I have been here a long time. This town may appear to be dying, but it really is filled with promise and wonderful men. If you're willing to settle here, I'm sure you can find a good husband to bring you happiness."

"It depends." Hester tilted her head to the side, a look on her face Jeddah didn't entirely understand. "I rather fancied the deputy, but he disappeared before I could get to know him better."

"Caleb is already spoken for," Jeddah snapped before remembering her promise to be more civil. "My friend, Daniella, and the deputy are betrothed."

"And the sheriff is recently married, too." Hester continued, nodding her understanding. "He would have been my second choice. I was getting so desperate, I even considered the mayor for a brief time."

"Just about any other man is town is a better choice," Jeddah blurted out, giggling at the suggestion any woman would consider the mayor a preference.

"I came to the same conclusion." Hester smiled. "After the third or fourth Sunday service, I saw you and the reverend holding hands. Something about the way he pulled you around after him as he greeted different people made me pause. Here I was, resenting you for misleading me into coming all this way in hopes of finding a rich husband, and I was missing the opportunity to find so much more."

"It only took you a few weeks to figure it out?" Jeddah fidgeted nervously with things around her. Someone had left a tattered hat in the pew. Another person had smudged the wooden handrail, and she took the edge of her skirt to remove it. Noah took pride in his church. Tidying up the area made her feel useful in a small way. "You're much wiser than I am, Hester. I'm still learning a lot of life's harder lessons. Thankfully, I have a wise man to help guide me."

"Success is measured in more than one way, isn't it? The mayor might be rich, but it would take a special woman to make him part with any of his money. The sheriff has power, but he's already married. The deputy has potential, but he's not around to claim."

"Mike Turner is a decent gentleman." Jeddah didn't think it wise to consider all the men who weren't available and began suggesting some who were.

Hester's voice changed as she spoke again, and it caught Jeddah's attention uncomfortably. "Noah might not be wealthy or be an elected official, but he has a level of power no one else in town does. People respect him. They listen to his words and weigh his advice. His wife will be in a position to influence life in this little town. One day, he will probably move to a better town, and his power—and his wife's—will only increase then."

It was the dreamy quality of Hester's voice which clued Jeddah in to the real meaning behind her words. Hester had already decided on a man to marry, and it was Noah.

Jeddah considered her answer carefully before speaking. "Being a minister's wife is not about having power. It's about many things, none of which involve using your husband's position to gain prestige. A woman would need to be willing to put her husband's needs above her own, to support him just as she does his ministry. Being a minister's wife means doing her best to take care of his family. It means helping him build his church, care for his followers, and live in a way which does not embarrass or dishonor him."

Laughing in a voice that grated, Hester stared Jeddah straight in the eye. "I'll bet he felt a bit dishonored when you stole his clothes. I heard him talking to the deputy, one day. They both had a good laugh about him having to preach in a pair of work breeches. In case you're wondering, that's when I decided to steal him from you." Another laugh followed. "Don't look at me like that, Jeddah. It's only fair, after all. You got me to follow you here. Why should you get to keep the only respectable man in town?"

Jeddah stared back with wide eyes. Would her past continue to haunt her? "Noah forgave me for taking his trousers, and we have moved past such nonsense. As for stealing him, he loves me. Do you really think you could get away with it?"

"Just watch me." The belittlement in Hester's voice was obvious as she adjusted the pleats in her skirt. "I offered to make him a new pair. You never did learn to sew more than a tea cloth, did you? I excel at the bothersome task, though. I started to list your shortcomings, along with your boastful letter, but he was quick to come to your defense. I realized you had already managed to win him over, so I changed my plans. The reverend has a soft heart for a tragic history. I had to invent an abusive father and brothers before he stopped pushing me away."

"Stay away from my man," Jeddah ordered. Noah was no match for the evil likes of Hester. Men were so blind when it came to selfish, controlling females.

"Nor did you bother to learn to cook, did you? I plan on

bringing him some of my home cooked food, next. It will be a bit overcooked, so I can pretend to panic about ruining perfectly good food. What do you think? Should I tell him my father broke my arm for burning a chicken? He might even examine my skin, when I tell him about all the scars I bear."

"I may find it hard to keep from giving you new ones," Jeddah's voice contained hurt and anxiousness. "Hester, I will not allow you to take advantage of Noah's giving, trusting nature."

"Oh, please do. It would give me an excuse to run to him and plead with him to protect me from you." Hester's eyes contained bitterness now. "From Jeddah, the evil woman who spews lies, steals other people's clothing, and attacks poor, helpless women."

"Noah will see through your deceit." Jeddah stood up and tried to keep her voice low.

"Oh? Like he saw through yours? You might want to set *your* sights on Mike Turner, because it's only a matter of time before Noah pushes you aside. For *me*." Hester stood up, as well, and took a threatening step toward Jeddah.

"Only a fool would push aside Jeddah Cromwell." A strong, deep male voice startled both women. They turned to see Noah had come back inside. His voice was stern. "And I am no fool. There is no other woman for me but Jeddah, nor will there ever be."

"Reverend Wilkins, I didn't see you come back. Jeddah cornered me after the services. She was upset because I told you about her letter back home." Hester's expression was so forlorn, Jeddah almost believed her.

"Might I suggest you save your home cooked efforts for your future husband? I hope you find a good, strong-willed man to help lead you along a better path in life. I'll pray for him. It's obvious to me, he'll need it." Noah offered his arm to Jeddah. "May I escort you back to the ranch, sweetheart? Faith invited me for lunch, and I hear there will be fried chicken."

Giving him a loving smile, Jeddah reached up to take his arm. But instead, he took her small hand into his and led her toward the doorway. She refused to even look back and tilted her head upward at Noah's indulgent smile.

"Yes, sir," she said. "And Aunt Faith promised to teach me how to prepare it just the way you like it."

## CHAPTER 10

AN EMPTY HEART...

*D*aniella had been at the brothel nearly three weeks. She stood in the kitchen peeling potatoes for supper as her thoughts of Caleb tortured her. She missed him so badly, it hurt. Was he still searching for her? Did his heart ache as much as hers? A tear slid down her cheek and landed in the bowl of water as she worked, splashing.

"Daniella," Madam Lydia's soft voice drew her back to the present. "Sit down. Let's have a cup of tea and a piece of Berthie's cake. You need to talk."

Daniella blinked away tears as she reached for a clean dish towel to dry her eyes. "Yes, ma'am. That would be lovely. But I really don't feel like talking."

"You may not feel like it, but you need to. Your heart is heavy; even I can see it."

Daniella watched as Lydia took the tea kettle off the stove, then she reached for the cups and saucers.

Lydia moved efficiently around the kitchen as she made tea and cut a generous piece of Berthie's chocolate cake for each of them.

"If Berthie complains because the cake is cut, tell her I did it." A gentle smile touched her face. "I have a story to tell you, Daniella. Sit."

Sitting, Daniella waited. It was a long time before Lydia spoke.

The soft hands poured the tea and set out the sugar bowl. "Once I was in love, too, Daniella. He was the most wonderful man I'd ever dreamed of. And I knew he loved me, too."

Alarmed brown eyes met green ones. "What happened?"

"We had an argument." Lydia stared down at the amber liquid in her cup, stirring the spoon gently. "I heard a rumor; one I found out later was untrue, and we had a terrible fight. We were to be married the next day. And I was so upset and so sure he didn't really love me, I left in the middle of the night."

Daniella watched her uncertainly. She had no idea what to say, and her voice had left her.

"It was weeks later when I found he'd come after me. But I managed to avoid him at every turn. I wanted to go back; I longed to, but I couldn't force myself to." A deep sadness overcame her. Finally, she leaned her chin on her hand and looked back at Daniella. "The point is, I could have turned things around, Daniella, but I didn't. It was one of the worst decisions of my entire life. By the time I awakened to my own foolishness, it was months later, and I learned he had given up on me and married someone else."

"Oh, ma'am, I'm so sorry."

"So am I. Not a day goes by that I don't regret leaving him. If I'd only turned around and gone back to him, my life would be so different today. I came here because I didn't know what else to do, just like you. Berthie, believe it or not, had money, and she took me in. She knew I was a virgin, but there were as few opportunities for a young woman who was desperate then as there are now." Lydia smiled. "No one else knows this, Daniella, but I'll tell you. Berthie is the real owner of this place. Not me. She insisted on an agreement. She lets me run it because I have good business sense, and she'd rather run her kitchen."

Daniella stared at her blankly. "Oh, Madam Lydia. I want to go back to Caleb. So much. But I don't even know if he'd have me now. He's likely gone home to Golden River and forgotten all about me."

"Would it be such a bad thing to go back to the ranch, yourself, and see? You aren't happy here; anyone can see it."

A sip of hot tea slid down Danny's throat, and she looked up. "Are you? Happy?"

Lydia's face blanched. She swallowed, as if the question was quite unexpected. "I've…adjusted to life here. No, I can't say I'm happy, exactly. But it's my life now. And it's of my own making. Don't do what I did, child. Go back to your husband before it's too late." Her emerald eyes sparkled with tears, and she patted Daniella's shoulder and rose, leaving the room.

Danny watched her go, her own tears flooding her face. Was it possible to go back?

She didn't know.

\* \* \*

Weeks had passed since Daniella had disappeared. Caleb had long since passed the frantic stage. He knew she hadn't gone back to Golden River; he'd have heard by now if she had. He'd convinced himself a thousand times that she'd been kidnapped or killed. The thought of it made him ill every time it entered his head. But he refused to give up.

He stood outside the church, with his hands jammed in his pockets, wondering where else he could go to look for Daniella. He nodded and tipped his hat toward an elderly lady as she passed, but his heart was filled with grief.

He'd kept returning to the hotel to see if she'd come back, but this morning, he had let the room go and decided to rent a sleeping room for a few days in the building next to the church. Danny wasn't coming back. He'd considered more than once, returning to Golden River, but he couldn't bring himself to leave Sacramento until he knew exactly where she was.

"No sign of her, lad?" a lilting voice at his elbow said, and he turned to glance at Father McKnight.

He shook his head. "No."

"Aye, well, I'm sorry. When she left, I thought I saw a look of determination in her eyes. She wanted to do everything in her power to be a good wife to ye."

Caleb turned to speak, but when he opened his mouth, nothing came out. The fight they'd had, the spanking he'd given her, he was unable to share with the priest.

Father McKnight nodded toward the ripped parchment that protruded from his pocket. "She did this?" At Caleb's nod, he shook his head. "Don't give up on her, lad. She loves ye."

Caleb fought the knot in his throat and, with a nod, moved past the priest and into the street.

The building at the end of the road caught his eye, and he stopped, staring at it. The brothel. It had no sign on it, but he knew what it was. The woman at the saloon had told him. It was the only place he hadn't been to.

Slowly putting one foot in front of the other, he moved toward it. If he found her there...if she'd been seeing other men... He couldn't finish the thought. Pressing his hand over the document in his pocket, he took another step, then another.

A moment later, he stood before the door and raised his fist to knock.

The door opened before he brought his knuckles down on it, and he stood there, face to face with a beautiful woman. She had a headful of red curls and striking green eyes.

"I'm afraid the girls are all busy at the moment, sir, but if you don't mind waiting—"

"I'm not here for that. I'm looking for a young lady who may have come in the past few weeks, seeking work. Small, brown hair, brown eyes."

Her eyes lit on the document in his pocket, and she paused, glancing up and down the street. "Come in, please," she said quietly, opening the door wide enough to admit him.

Caleb entered. The inside parlor was dimly lit but well enough he could see around him. It was decorated with lush velvets and appeared grand.

"Tell me more about the young woman you're looking for," she said softly, "and please, sit down."

Caleb balked but, eventually, sat in one of the chairs, and she settled on the sofa not far away, her hands clasped in her lap. She looked out of place for this kind of setting.

He frowned, taking the parchment from his pocket. "She's my wife."

Her eyes widened as he pulled it out in two pieces. She glanced at him with a frown, before taking it from his grasp and examining it. It was torn between the signatures, as if to separate them forever. She sat for a moment, staring at it. Finally, she handed it back. "I might know where she is."

Caleb tried to hide his determination. "She's here, then?"

She leaned back. "I said *might*. Did you tear this up?"

"No." He kept his voice low, wondering why he was sharing this with a woman he'd never met. "*She* did."

They stared at each other for a moment. Finally, she gave him a soulful glance. "I have reason to know she cares for you. Very much."

"And I love her," he said, taking the parchment back and carefully tucking it into his pocket. "Please, tell me she's safe. And she isn't hungry or afraid…" A strangled sound made its way into his voice. "And tell me she hasn't been seeing other men."

"And if she has?"

Alarm filled his face. "Then, I think I might have to kill them."

She was staring back at him, her chin held high. "Times are hard for a young woman with no means of support, Mr. Matthews. They have little choice when they come to a place like this." She observed him for a moment and finally smiled. "But, no, she hasn't. However, I'll let her share that with you." She rose gracefully and moved to the inner door. Opening it, she looked inside. "Where's Daniella? There's a gentleman here to see her. Go get her, please, Leanna."

Caleb watched as she turned back to face him.

"Please wait here, Mr. Matthews." And she disappeared.

~

*L*eanna nodded demurely at Madam Lydia. She was cautious never to show her true, jaded nature in front of the lady who ran the brothel. Lydia was unlike any madam Leanna had ever encountered. For someone who rented out her rooms to ladies plying their trade, Lydia had a sense of honor and decency, which was hard to comprehend. She no doubt believed all the nonsense Mr. Matthews had just proclaimed, but Leanna was wiser to the faults of men.

As she left to find Daniella, she wondered if Madam Lydia was sending the poor girl to sure heartbreak. Leanna had come to depend on the new 'boy' who worked at the house. Daniel could create the most wonderful outfits, though 'he' blushed when asked to leave out the crotches. What a waste! Now, the dutiful little wife would spend all her days sewing bland clothes for her no-good husband and a wagon load of kids.

*Unless*…a shy smile played across her lips as she found Daniella peeling apples in the kitchen all alone. "We have a new customer in the parlor, Daniel. Which costume should I wear to entertain him?"

Daniella's face turned crimson. Even in old pants and a shirt, Leanna did not think anyone could mistake her as a boy. She and the other girls had known it from the start. The girl's hips were too full, her eyelashes too lush, and her breasts too perky.

Even her voice was utterly feminine. "I'm sure your new friend will enjoy either of the two outfits you had made."

Smiling, Leanna began to scheme. It would be perfect if she could plan things carefully enough so she could keep her seamstress and send the evil husband packing. She remembered learning Daniella's man was a deputy and decided to use that information to her advantage. "I wish I had gotten you to make me a bank robber outfit. My new friend loves to wrestle with outlaws."

The knife in Daniel's hand slipped and she nicked her finger. Grabbing a rag, she tried to stem the flow of blood and act unconcerned, but Leanna noticed.

Daniella's voice sounded husky and soulful. "A lawman... Has your sheriff friend come back to visit?"

"Not the sheriff. This man is a deputy...all the way from Golden River, I hear. He did have a strange request, though. He wanted me to dress up as a virginal bride. Maybe you can give me some pointers on how to act." Leanna watched Daniella grab the knife again and decided to change tactics. This little bride looked like she would slice open any woman who tried to bed her man.

Taking a step back, she eyed the knife in Daniella's hand.

"Listen Daniel, I have a marvelous idea. I could dress you up and allow you to entertain him. You could tease him, test how far he wants to play out his fantasy, and step outside before any real naughty stuff happens. I can take over from there."

∼

*D*aniella forced herself to stop gripping the knife as a weapon. Leanna was likely lying. Caleb would never come to a brothel. Then she recalled seeing him all those days ago. He looked so lost and lonely. Had she pushed him to this point? Could he really be here, hoping to enjoy one night of passion to remember his failed marriage? He said he could hardly recall the details of their lovemaking. She cleared her throat, trying to sound unconcerned.

"I think your new friend might find it strange that a kitchen 'boy' wanted to spend time with him upstairs." She went back to her apple. The skin was gone, but she continued hacking away at the meat now. Even in boy's clothes, he would recognize her.

Setting the knife down carefully, she studied the remains of the apple. But her thoughts were on Caleb. Was he really here? How she wished she could be with him, one last time. However, she knew, if he recognized her, he'd only feel honor-bound to haul her back home with him. No. It would kill her, but she would stay in the kitchen until he left.

"I don't think so, Leanna."

"Oh, I could fix you up so no one would know who you are. I have a wig, all the way from back east, made from the finest horse hair. It's dyed white and will give you an air of mystery. You can wear the masque I had made for the masquerade ball I went to a few years ago. He'll never know you. Weren't you making a white gown for one of the other girls? I bet you would look fetching in it."

Daniella recalled the dress she had just finished hemming that morning. "It's sheer!" she protested. "Even with a shift on, I'd feel naked."

"That's the general idea," Leanna beamed.

Before she could protest, Daniella found herself led to the upstairs of the house and painted up to look like a doll. A heavy wig styled in a manner which was all the rage back east a few decades before was slapped on her head. Her clothes were yanked and pulled off, and a thin, see-through, white slip was pulled over her head. Then her feet were shoved into slippers which were too big for her.

"You said the deputy was looking for a virginal bride," she groused. "I feel just the opposite."

Leanna stared at Daniella thoughtfully, considering her own intentions. "Look, Daniella. I'm sorry. I've changed my mind. I think you should make your own decisions about your future. Will you decide to go back to the husband you adore so much? Or will you decide to stay? I don't know. In truth, I'd hate to see you go. You really are quite the seamstress, and you work hard at making the outfits the ladies here desire. In addition, you cook and clean and help do whatever anyone asks of you. It would be a shame to have you leave."

Finally, the woman sighed and nodded. "As much as I would hate to lose you, I won't rob you of control of your own fate. The man downstairs is the brute who broke you heart, isn't he? This is your chance to see if he really loves you, pet. Go in there as Ella, the brothel's newest lady of ill repute. Test how faithful and loving your man really is when he doesn't think you're near."

Daniella's eyes grew wide. "I couldn't do that," she whispered.

"Sure you can. Taunt him. Seduce him. Make him work to please you. If he makes love to you, it's another memory of sex to take with you into your old age, for I fear you are one of those women destined to only give your love to one man. If he turns you away, you can pull off the wig, wipe your face clean, and give him a second chance. What is there to lose?"

Daniella battled with her thoughts, wondering if she dared to try following such an outrageous plan. The younger, wilder Danny who had come out west would have thrilled at such an opportunity. She could pretend to be a wanton woman, yet secretly remain faithful to her own man. She frowned, remembering a time or two when Caleb caught her taking wild risks like the one she was considering. He did not approve of her wilder tendencies.

But when—*when* would she ever get another chance like this? Her current path promised a lifetime of living off the memory of one lovemaking session. Caleb had told her it only hurt the first time. Didn't she deserve a second opportunity to see if he was being honest?

She would do it. Daniella stood up and steeled her courage. "I'll do it," she whispered. "But how do I stop him from recognizing my voice?"

"Lower your tone to a whisper. Keep it husky. Men love the sound," Leanna advised and moved to the shutters to dim the light in her bedroom. "Keep it dark in here. It will play into the shy virgin act. Let him do most of the talking, but don't make it easy for him. Make him beg. Balk at his size. Men have a need to feel impressive about the length of their private region. Insist it won't fit. Demand a chance to study him to gauge how large it is, then make sure your hot breath touches it every chance you can. Open your mouth and take the very tip inside, as if you are seeing what it might feel like inside you."

A small gasp escaped Daniella's throat. "I don't know if I could do that, even for my Caleb. Ladies just don't do such things. If I did, he might never want me for a wife. This might not be such a good idea."

"And one more thing." Leanna reached into the drawer and pulled out a piece of brown paper. When she unfolded it, she held out a delicate white satin masque with ribbons fastened to the sides. It was lovely. "Turn around," she ordered. "Let's see how this fits you."

Daniella pivoted to glance at herself in the mirror as Leanna tied the ribbons behind her head. With the wig and the mask partially hiding her face, it just might be possible to prevent Caleb from knowing her. She barely recognized herself.

Shoving her down on the bed, Leanna pushed aside her objections. "Trust me, pet, a man would think he had died and gone to heaven if you acted like the proper wife in public and a wanton brothel worker in private. If you decide to keep him, anyway. This is about you deciding what you want, Daniella. Not many of us get a chance to decide our own future, so make us proud."

Lying in the bed, Daniella attempted to scratch her scalp without upsetting the wig. Horse hair might look like natural hair, but it was uncomfortable and hard to keep in place. Part of her feared Caleb would recognize her the moment he walked in the room. If so, he'd feel honor-bound to take her back home with him, and she would always wonder how he really felt about her. She couldn't stand the thought of being married to the man she loved, knowing she was a mistake he had to learn to cope with. If only she knew how he really, truly felt about her. Did he love her, even a tiny bit? If he could undo their one night of passion, would he do it just to avoid being trapped in an unhappy marriage?

Voices outside the door reached her ears suddenly, and she stiffened. It was Caleb, arguing with Leanna, and he was not happy. She was filled with regret.

"I don't care if I would be the only man to claim this young lady. Madam Lydia promised to deliver the woman I asked for when I arrived. No one else will do."

The door flew open, and she saw her husband's tall shadow fill the frame. He stared at her, lying on the bed, for a long time. Her legs had been spread open when Leanna had shoved her down. She quickly closed them and tried to affect a more seductive image. An awkward silence followed, and he started at her head and worked his way forward slowly. "And if you lied about me being the only man to have her, you'll be sorry. *And* your madam."

"And Ella?" Leanna asked in a snide tone. "Will you hurt her, too? Because I won't allow any harm to come to her, nor will the other people who work here."

"Aside from a reddened backside, *Ella* will always be safe with me." He turned to stare Leanna into backing up a few steps and slammed the door closed between them. Twisting the key in the lock, he listened for the click, then tossed the key on the highboy.

He advanced to the bed slowly, tugging at his clothes as he went. "How many men have you entertained since coming here?" he demanded. Even in the dark, she could feel the anger of his stare.

"None!" she called out quickly then remembered to change her voice. "I haven't been upstairs until now. Leanna said you wanted a certain type of…friend to entertain you."

He stopped to regard her again. "And will you entertain me, little Ella? Will you let me lie against you and pump my seed deep inside you? What if I want to pretend you are my runaway bride? I have had a strong yearning to turn someone's backside bright red for torturing me, for weeks now. How much extra would it cost me to take my frustration out on your soft, perfect little bottom?"

She gulped. "Your bride—ran away from you?" Daniella tried to forge surprise. *Did he recognize her?* Should she admit everything and beg for forgiveness? Leanna's suggestion about determining her own fate rang in her ears. She would see this through to the end. "What a foolish girl. After the punishment, will there be pleasure? The cost will be higher if you leave without comforting."

His belt made a hissing sound as he pulled it from his trousers. "Oh, I can offer pleasure you will never find with another man, and that, dear Ella, is a promise."

Caleb stood there, his belt in his hand, staring at her. Her eyes were wide, her shoulders stiff, as if she were terribly frightened. The sheer gown she wore hid very little. Neither did the white masque. Those eyes—those brown gorgeous eyes of hers that peeked through, there was no mistaking. He had a strong inclination to use the belt he'd just pulled from his trousers across her bare bottom for all the pain and worry she'd caused him the past few weeks. At the same time, he wanted to take her in his arms and just hold her and comfort her. She'd seen the harsh side of him too much, already.

The belt dropped to the floor. She watched it land with obvious relief in her eyes and then slowly, warily, raised them to his.

"Where have you been?" He knew his voice was husky, but so was hers when she answered.

"I..."

She looked at a loss for words, and those big brown eyes suddenly couldn't meet his. "Here, But I don't...work up here in the rooms."

"Then, where do you work?" He approached the bed as he spoke.

Her eyes grew wider. "Downstairs...

Another step brought him still closer. "And what do you do...*downstairs*?" His voice was softer now.

"I sew and help in the kitchen." The whisper in her voice was softer, her eyes wider, watching him. "And help out in the garden."

"I see."

He was standing over her now, moving closer. Not wishing to frighten her further, he slowed his movements. They would be alone now, and he knew he could take his time. At last, he'd found her. And with her trapped under him, she wasn't going anywhere. "Tell me, little one, what do you want from your husband?"

Recognition flashed in those eyes. Did she know he recognized her? She had to, surely.

Her voice was husky but definitely Daniella's. "Patience," she whispered. "Kindness. And love." The last word had been strangled. Her eyes were misty now. *Oh, God, she was going to cry.*

He leaned down over her and kissed the tear that trickled down her cheek. "Shhh, don't cry. It'll be all right, I promise. It would be impossible for any man not to love you."

A hiccup escaped from her, followed by a whisper, and she met his eyes. "Are you sure?"

He lowered further, kissing first her nose, then her forehead; then giving her a long look, he brought his mouth down on hers once, twice. His tongue descended into her mouth, and she eagerly took it, inviting, dancing.

"Have you any idea how beautiful you are?" A slow growl erupted from him. He caressed her softly with his hands and framed her face. "Talk to me. Tell me what you want from me."

She looked up, confused. "But I told you."

He shook his head. "No. You said you wanted someone kind and patient, who would love you. What do you want from me right now?" His thumb ran gently down her cheek. "Right this moment?"

Even in the darkness, she blushed delicately, and he smiled. "My shy little girl."

"I'm not a lit—" It was as far as he allowed her to get before he covered her mouth with his.

"No," he said softly in her ear, "you certainly aren't." Rising to his knees, he turned her onto her belly and brought the curls from the wig to one side. Smiling, he watched her profile. The wig was far less beautiful than her real hair; he'd much preferred to have her long tresses trailing down her back to play with. These days with her gone had left him thinking about her. Some of their lovemaking right before the wedding had made its way back into his mind. Her hair had curled gently down the sides of her face and onto her shoulders that night. He wanted to see it now, just like that.

"Take off this ridiculous wig," he said in her ear. "I want to see your real hair."

Immediately, she stiffened. "I—don't know what you mean, sir."

Caleb leaned down and gave her a nip on the back of her neck, and she gave a slight squeal. *So this was the way she wanted to play it?* How could she possibly think he hadn't recognized her? He shook his head and moved a little lower, down her back. He hadn't even undressed her yet, nor himself. Slowly, he kissed his way down through the sheer gown, until he reached the crease of her bottom, then moved lower until he found himself at the top of her thighs. Reaching for the tail of her gown, he brought it up very slowly, running his hands along the inside of her thighs. It was the slightest whisper of a touch, but those velvety legs leading to such a soft bottom caused him to nearly be undone. He stopped, closing his eyes to regain composure, before continuing to bring it further upward, exposing her tiny waist and her back. The soft mounds of her breasts, he could see peeking out below her. His hands paused there, caressing, and she let out a soft groan of delight.

Caleb's guttural growl, he couldn't prevent. But he was determined to be slow and patient, even if it killed him.

And it very likely would.

He brought the gown up, first removing one arm from it, then the other. She gave soft little cries of pleasure as he brought it over her head. Careful not to disturb the absurd wig, he turned her onto her back.

Face to face with her beautiful breasts, he leaned down to take them into his mouth, one at a time. She was so perfect. He sucked lightly on first one, then the other, feeling them pebble in his mouth. She made a soft moan, and unable to prevent it, another low growl escaped him.

It was when he raised himself up over her to kiss her, he saw it, that adorable little dimple she possessed. Sometimes, there were two, but the appearance of one from her left cheek always symbolized mischief at having accomplished something. In this case, perhaps she thought she'd fooled him? His expression changed suddenly, and hers became wary.

Purposely, he allowed a smile to cross his face. Outsmarted him? For now, he'd let her think she had. His pace increased, however, and he stepped up his lovemaking a bit and his roughness just a little. When he glanced down at his belt on the floor, he noticed how full of trepidation she became. The dimple had disappeared completely. He was tempted to retrieve it, put her naked over his knee, and redden that gorgeous little bottom with it. But not yet.

Not yet.

Leaning down, he moved to her bud and began to suck gently. He reached inside her with a hooked finger and tickled the front of her channel with it, tapping, and she closed her eyes and stiffened.

Suddenly, she flew apart. A low wail escaped as she cried out in bliss and her body responded. Caleb stared down at the magnificent reaction she had to his lovemaking. Had she done this the last time they made love? How could he have not managed to remember it? My God, if the alcohol had blocked out the orgasm from his memory, he'd never touch another drop. This was amazing.

Her gaze up at him now drew him in, as if she would be totally faithful to him the rest of her life.

He moved upward, his face inches from hers. "You are so beautiful," he said softly, kissing away the tears that escaped under the masque.

"You..." she whispered softly, "you're still dressed."

He answered with a half-smile and allowed her to begin pushing his trousers downward. Once he had one knee out, he kicked the garment to the floor but brought her to another peak before he brought his shaft to the outside of her channel. Meeting her eyes, he waited until she nodded before entering as gently as he could.

Suddenly, she began to weep.

He stopped. "What is it, my love?"

But she only shook her head and bit her lip.

"Am I hurting you?" His voice was as gentle as he could make it. She shook her head and looked away. "Oh, no. Eyes on me," he said, a stern sound creeping into his voice. When she tried to avoid him, he took her face into his hands. "Only me." he said, his voice firmer than it previously was.

She gulped and brought those beautiful eyes back up to meet his, swallowing hard. She'd spoken very little but looked as if she was about to start sobbing.

"Shhh, my girl. I'll be gentle, if that's what frightens you."

"No," she whispered. "That's not it."

He was inside her now. "Then, what is it?"

She lifted her hips off the bed, trying to meet his, and he thrust. Her moan of pleasure answered, and he moved inside her again. What began as slow and rhythmic quickly turned to faster and firmer thrusts. He kept her eyes trained on his as he fought to prolong his own pleasure, and she came apart once again, just as he did.

Cries filled the room, hers, a soft series of moans, his, a series of deep guttural sounds that he couldn't stop. It seemed to go on forever, until finally, he cradled her in his arms and brought her back against his chest, reveling in the feel of her soft skin against his.

Realizing the ribbon to the masque had come undone, he leaned over her to observe that perfect little profile he'd grown to love. She hadn't even realized the masque lay on the pillow beside her. Her eyes were closed, but he doubted she was asleep. Kissing her temple, he smiled.

"Sleep, my love," he whispered in her ear as he cocooned himself around her small body. He'd found her, and he would never let her go.

Eventually, he allowed his eyes to close. And he slept.

## CHAPTER 11

*How* could he?

Daniella lay quietly in the arms of her husband, trying desperately to keep from sobbing. He hadn't recognized her, yet he allowed himself to make love to someone in her place? How could he! She willed her shoulders not to shake, failing only once. When his arms tightened around her, she forced herself into composure and lay still.

He'd betrayed her. Anger filled her down to her toes. But at the same time, so much regret. Oh, God, what a fool she'd been to leave him in the first place! She'd given him no choice but had effectively removed herself from his life. If she'd stayed, she might have begun to woo him back to her. He'd been so gentle as a lover. Yet he'd seemed so angry when he had come in. He'd held the belt in his hands, and she'd been so sure he was going to use it. And yet, he hadn't. What had changed his mind?

She'd always known he could be a gentle man if he wanted. All this time, since the very first moment she'd seen him standing in the river waters, naked, she'd thought about what it would be like to be loved by him. Now, she knew. It was wonderful. And it was terrible, at the same time. This would be the last time he would have the chance. And she had only herself to blame.

When his soft snoring echoed in her ear, she pulled away slightly. Caleb didn't move. It was then, and only then, that she allowed her shoulders to shake with silent sobs. She must not awaken him. She had to get away.

Naked, she slowly and silently reached for the key and eased it into the lock. She cringed as the click sounded, looking back over her shoulder. But Caleb still didn't move. Tiptoeing out-side, she looked up and down the hallway, wondering if she could make it downstairs without being seen.

As she looked back into the bedroom one more time, she saw it. One of the pieces of parchment she'd torn in half to separate their two signatures lay on the floor. Not knowing what made her do it, she crept back in and picked it up.

It wasn't the one with her signature on it. No, it contained Caleb's handwriting, *his* name.

Pressing it to her chest, she began once again to sob and ran from the room and down the steps.

~

"Daniella? It's me, Leanna. I'm coming in."

Danny could not control the gut-wrenching sobs pouring from her now. She didn't even look up as Leanna walked up behind her and put a hand on her shoulder.

"How could he?" Daniella wept.

"I'm sorry, pet." Leanna's voice was comforting.

Pulling away, she tried to calm herself and failed. Still sobbing, she moved to the bed and sat down. Caleb could not be the man she had always thought him to be. Her man would never betray her this way. Making love to another woman, even if it was really his own wife the entire time, was an unforgiveable sin. "Married men don't visit brothels and make sweet, passionate love to strangers!" The words escaped her lips before she could stop them. Leanna didn't say a word to contradict her, but Danny knew she probably wanted to laugh aloud at the absurd comment.

The memory of the sheriff's departure from the brothel the very day she arrived had Danny cursing her own naïve beliefs. Obviously, some men did, but not her perfect, respectable, loyal Caleb. In her heart, she was sure he had been faithful to her from the moment they first met. How did she reconcile this new knowledge —with the man she loved above all others?

Maybe he didn't consider it as a betrayal? She had vanished on him, leaving him a message to tell him their marriage was not valid and he was free to have it annulled. Had he? A loud gasp escaped between her tears as she flung herself on top of the bed. Had Caleb taken her up on the suggestion to have Father void the vows? The man she loved was perfect in her eyes, but he did have limits to his patience. He had tried to put distance between them, and she had followed him here. He wanted to wait to get married; she all but dragged him to the church. He ordered her to stay put in the hotel, but she ran away.

She had done everything in her power to push him away. No wonder he turned to another woman's bed. At least with a woman at a brothel, a man knew what was expected. The women there did not chase after men, demanding a commitment!

"I can't stay here now. It's only a matter of time before Caleb knows I'm here."

The mattress sagged a bit as Leanna sat down beside her. "This is all my fault. Getting you to wear the wig and dress up like someone else was foolish. My impulsive behavior rushed ahead of good sense. At first, I thought to give you a chance to test your husband and make sure he really deserved your love. All I ended up doing was destroying your future. Tell me how I can make things better."

"I have to go home." Danny thought for a while before turning over to face her. "I have to. Staying here is not an option now. I hardly have enough money to take a stage coach to the nearest train station." The sobbing has stopped, but tears continued to slide down her pale cheeks.

"Before you decide if that really is the path you want to choose, you need to consider the chance... Forgive me for asking, but did you and your husband?" Leanna seemed undecided about what she meant to say. "You need to wait a few weeks before you head home. I know your family loves you, but what if you turn up expecting, after today? Your family might well throw you out, instead of dealing with the shame."

Danny heard something strange in Leanna's tone, as if she was speaking from personal experience. Wiping aside her tears, she began to question Leanna about it. "Did your family turn you out?"

Leanna's eyes misted, but she did not speak.

Waiting a few weeks more might be prudent, Danny realized. Acting rashly, at this point, could have dire consequences for more than just herself. The mere notion made her feel nauseous. How long would it take before she could determine if Caleb's seed had taken root inside her? What signs should she be on the watch for?

"How would a woman know she was expecting?" she asked.

"It varies from one to another," Leanna said, patting her hand. "Some don't know until months later, though I would think missing your monthly would be a sure sign. Others seem to know right away. They get all weepy without cause. I knew when my breasts started growing tender..." Leanna's mouth snapped shut.

Danny barely noticed. She was too concerned with pressing her hands against her chest. Earlier, when Caleb had made sweet love to her, she had almost protested when he suckled her nipples. She started counting back to her last monthly, and with each week she noted, her stomach lurched. "Oh, Leanna. I don't have to wait weeks to find out. The night before we were married, Caleb and I... but it was only once. I was terrified I might conceive and rushed off to hunt down someone to marry us. Caleb was so mad. He looked at me as if I had betrayed him."

"Listen to me carefully, Daniella." Leanna's expression grew serious. "If you are, don't do anything rash. Trust me, only heartache follows. We need to take our time and consider what is best. I will help you any way I can. I am sure Madam Lydia will want to help, too. You wait here, and I'll go fetch her." Leanna stood at the door for a long time before she took a deep breath and opened it.

Danny waited until she heard the resounding click. Danny pictured her father's face if she arrived home without a husband, carrying a baby. He barely had money to feed his own children and had sent her out west to ease his burden. Her mother would never believe she had married the father of her child. She searched the room for the half of the parchment she had taken from Caleb, a moment before. Scooping it up, she didn't even take the time to pack up her meager belongings. She'd arrived with only the clothes on her back, and she retrieved them, pulling them on as quickly as she could.

Rushing to the window, she was glad Madam Lydia had given her a room on the bottom floor. She climbed out and started dashing blindly away from the house. Berthie hobbled out of the stable, and Danny impulsively ran up to hug her. "Thank you, Berthie, for everything you've done. Please tell the others? I'm sorry."

"Tell them yourself, girl. We'll be sharing a meal in a few hours." The old woman, not one to accept affection gracefully, pulled free and headed toward the house.

"Please forgive me," Danny muttered desperately. Walking to Golden River was impossible. It would take hours to get where she was heading. There was only one place in the world she could seek shelter now. "I hope they don't hang horse thieves out here," she muttered and rushed inside the stable. "Once I get where I'm going, I'll have one of the ranchers take you back." She hefted the worn-out saddle onto the mare's back and tugged hard. Madam Lydia would surely hate her for stealing the only horse she owned. "Perhaps they can get you back home even before anyone notices you're gone."

∼

"Be still, Araminta." Lydia frowned, standing inside the next bedroom, helping her dress. She paused in the process of lacing up the red corset the moment she heard the click of the door down the hall. A few seconds later, Leanna passed the door of Araminta's room, wearing a devious expression. Trying not to groan, Lydia hoped a disaster was not about to befall them as she stepped toward the door. Raising her voice was unusual for her, but she did. "Leanna?"

The hiss as Leanna sucked in her breath was clearly heard. She, too, paused in the hallway.

Lydia intentionally softened her voice. "Araminta, go ask Nellie Ann or Charlotte to help you finish dressing. Both should be available. There are no gentlemen callers here at the moment."

She stepped outside the room as the blue-eyed Araminta began to protest. However, she stopped short. They both stared at Leanna as she turned to face them.

Araminta shook her head. "Don't forget your promise, Madam Lydia."

Lydia tried to hide her frustration. As if she could forget her foolish promise. She'd sworn to the rest of the girls she would turn the troublemaker out if she continued to cause turmoil. Since the very beginning of her stay, Leanna managed to cause one bout of mischief after another, and everyone was tired of it. Araminta scooted away to find one of the other girls to help. Lydia doubted it was so they could help her finish dressing. No, they all would want to witness the brat finally getting her just reward. Pinching the bridge of her nose and praying for patience, Lydia hoped she would not have to toss the poor girl out. She hated turning her back on any woman in need, even if she deserved it.

"Please don't tell me you have only just gotten around to fetching Danny. I sent you off more than an hour ago," Lydia demanded, crossing her hands under her bosom. Leanna stared back at her, her face blanched, and Lydia continued. "Am I to assume your guilty expression is the result of me catching you off guard, or is there something else you'd like to confess?"

Leanna's face crumpled, and she began to wail, "Oh, Madam Lydia. You will never forgive me."

Now, Lydia was truly concerned. Leanna's tears were genuine. Worse, she was not trying to deny things. "Leanna? What have you done, this time? I've never seen you in this state." Guilt? She'd never thought this girl capable of such an emotion.

Leanna's voice dropped to little above a whisper as she explained how she'd set Daniella up to play the virgin bride and then brought in Caleb to her room. "I'm sorry," she said tearfully. "I didn't want to lose her!"

Lydia shook her head. "I'm sure you didn't. She sews for you, she cooks and cleans, so you don't have to lift a finger. But that isn't the question. The question is why didn't you do as I asked and just bring her to the parlor?"

Leanna wiped her eyes. "I don't know. And now, she wants to leave, and I don't know what to do. I've ruined—"

Lydia glanced, alarmed, toward Daniella's closed door. Putting a hand to her head, she turned toward the room. "I'll speak to her."

It was then that Berthie entered the darkened hallway, looking baffled. "I just had the strangest conversation with Daniella. She kissed my cheek and said, 'I'm sorry, Berthie,'"

Lydia's eyes grew wider, and she ran for Danny's room.

"Where?" shouted Leanna.

"Just outside the stables."

Without a word, Leanna ran for the kitchen and the back door. But thirty seconds later, she was back. "She's gone!" she said, holding her side and bending forward from effort. "And she's taken Speed with her!"

∽

$\mathcal{C}$aleb slowly crawled back from the depth of sleep, smiling, and let out a long sigh of contentment. He finally had his little wife in his arms again. He opened his eyes and looked down. The smile vanished.

Daniella was gone.

He stared at the empty spot where she'd lain, just moments before, as if he had difficulty comprehending her absence.

"Daniella?"

No answer. He rose up on one elbow, staring around the room. "Daniella?" He lowered his hand to the spot next to him where she'd rested. It was cold.

Her sheer gown caught his eye, followed by the wig and mask. Like a shot, he was out of bed, grabbing his trousers and struggling to get his feet into them without falling and breaking his neck. He managed to get the right one on. Shouting at the top of his lungs, he waited for an answer. There was none. He thought, however, he could hear female voices downstairs. Pausing at the door, he reached for his shirt and left boot, and without thinking, felt of his pocket for the parchment, just as he had for the past several weeks. Finding it empty, he looked frantically around the room. There was something rolled up, on the floor, just under the bed, and he dived for it.

It was her half of their marriage license, the half with her own neat script on it. She'd taken his half?

What the hell?

Caleb tucked the parchment back into his pocket and the boot under his arm and raced down the stairs, taking them three at a time.

He found them all in the parlor, staring at each other and talking rapidly. Throwing the door open, he demanded an explanation.

"Where is she?"

*L*ydia, standing in the center of the room, was pressing her hands to her ears as shrieks filled the air. But before Caleb could speak again, the chatter once again began.

"How could you do that to our little Danny," a dark headed young woman demanded.

"She's not wise to the world like you are, Leanna!"

And yet a third. "You have no idea what you've done! She loved her husband!" One voice after another filled the parlor as Lydia held out a hand to silence them.

It did no good. The chatter was at a fevered pitch now, and Caleb found himself unable to understand any of it.

Finally, an older woman raised a hand in the air. "Stop! You're saying she stole the horse? We take the child in, and she repays us by stealing our only horse?"

Caleb lowered himself into a chair but only long enough to shove on his other boot. Looking from one to another, he stood once again and fastened his shirt, patting the pocket. It did not go unnoticed on Lydia.

Their eyes met, and Caleb nodded, jerking open the front door.

"You'll catch her," Lydia assured him as he left. "Speed is the slowest animal on the face of the earth. But she'll get Daniella safely back home."

Caleb had the reins in his hands now, but he could still hear the voices from inside. Madam Lydia's rose above the rest of them now. "Berthie? Take the stew off the stove. Ladies, to town. We need to find a wagon to get us to Golden River."

~

*A*n hour later, luck was with them. All six ladies piled in the back of a wagon driven by a man who called himself Mike Turner. He appeared genuinely surprised when Lydia approached him to ask if he'd transport them, but he readily agreed. There was another man there who introduced himself as Mayor Blackaby, from Golden River, and Leanna looked impressed.

Lydia leaned over into Leanna's face as they bumped along slowly.

"You'd better thank the powers that be. I think the girls were ready to scratch your eyes out for this."

Leanna leaned back. "I said I was sorry."

The commotion in the wagon rose, and Lydia turned back to face the rest of the ladies. "Think about this," she appealed. "Please, everyone stop and take a moment to think logically. It is safe to assume, even dressed up in a costume, a man would be able to recognize his own wife. Continue explaining, Leanna. What happened next?"

"But he didn't seem to. I mean, I wasn't there, but..." Leanna propped her head over one of the madam's shoulders and glared at the other girls. "Even with the wig and make up and the masque I put on her, you'd think her husband would know who she was. I did tell her to change her voice a bit and gave her the masque, so perhaps he wouldn't. And of course, it was dark in the room—"

Bedlam broke loose again, and it took several precious minutes to pull off the hands which were wrapped tightly around the culprit's slender neck. Even Berthie was in the fray.

Mike pulled the wagon to a halt. He jumped down to the ground, his large frame as imposing as he could make it. The next thing Leanna knew, she was hoisted out of the wagon and brought to the buckboard to sit by Blackaby. Lydia was next, and he put her next to him, setting her down with a distinct thud. "If you two so much as look at each other, there'll be hell to pay," he declared.

Turning to the other girls, he said, "Not one more word, any of you. Or you can walk all the rest of the way to Golden River. If you're going to kill each other, do it in someone else's wagon." With that, he jumped back into the wagon and whistled for the horses.

Not another sound was heard from any of them. And the rest of the way, calm, cool, and elegant Lydia tried desperately to recall what had made her decide to choke the life out of Leanna. This was so unlike her. But with Mike Turner sitting next to her and glaring down at her every few seconds, it was hard to concentrate on anything else but those stern brown eyes.

For the life of her, she just couldn't remember.

# CHAPTER 12

TO FACE THE MUSIC...

*D*anny poured her heart out to Speed as she constantly urged her to go faster. She had to talk to someone, and the mare was the only beast there with ears.

"And my monthly is late, Speed. So, returning to my home back east is impossible. My poor father would be dreadfully disappointed in me, and mother doesn't need two more mouths to feed. They are already responsible for too many as it is. It wouldn't be fair to add to their burden." She was sobbing now, using the back of her hands to push away the tears that blurred her vision. "I don't suppose you have any words of wisdom to share?"

But Speed, Madam Lydia's old, lazy mare, trudged along, unimpressed with the human astride her.

"Still upset with me for taking you away from your oat sack?" she cajoled. "I promise to feed you as soon as you help me reach home. And then you can return to your stall at home. I'll try to get someone to take you back." She was examining the landscape as they moved, hoping for something she recognized. When a familiar patch of land appeared in the distance ahead, she grew excited.

"We must be on the right path back to Golden River!" But a moment later, her expression changed. What if, she fretted, they were traveling in a huge circle. But, no, surely not. She shook her head after a moment of despair, refusing to give in to the urge to break down and lose all hope. She patted Speed's sweaty neck and urged her to pick up the pace a little.

Dear God, I do hope we aren't lost, she prayed silently.

If it was even possible, Speed slowed further, and Danny began talking again, non-stop. "Caleb is probably waking up, this very moment. Don't be surprised if he sneaks up on us. He's bound to yell and put up a fuss about me running away from him again, but he's an honest man, Speed. A decent man. You never got to meet him, so you'll have to take my word for his character. He takes care of his own. I don't doubt for a minute that he'll track me down someday soon, especially if he suspects I might be carrying his child. He'll want to honor his duty, you see. I'm sure he's been looking for me."

A new flow of tears began pouring forth, and she tried to dash them away. "It's my fault he turned into a such an unfaithful bastard," she blurted out. "I still can't believe he did it."

Speed gave a soft whinny of sympathy, and Danny wiped her tears, trying to clear her vision. "Of course, he wasn't *really* unfaithful, since it was *me* he took to bed." A hand flew to her mouth. "Oh! I wonder if he paid money!" Vehemently, she shook her head, sending her long curls flying. "*No!* I won't think of such things right now. I *won't!*"

She noticed suddenly the quiet path seemed to grow even more quiet. Moments before, birds flew overhead and small creatures scampered about in the trees and fields. Had she spooked the wildlife away with her weeping?

When she'd first come to the west, she'd longed for chances like this. Having the opportunity to explore the treasures and mystery of this untamed land had consumed all her waking moments since the first news of the gold rush had come east. She'd learned to scour the local newspaper, searching for adventure in the west.

Now, however, her only desire was to find a nice, quiet spot to consider her future.

For the tenth time, she struggled to keep Speed on the established path—the path she hoped would lead her back to the ranch at Golden River. Speed was beautiful, but she had to be the slowest creature Daniella had ever encountered. For pity's sake, she might get there sooner walking than to rely on this old mare for transportation. She seemed to have neither the energy nor the desire to go any faster.

The mare gave a start, suddenly, and Danny grabbed her mane to hold on. "Why are you acting so skittish?" she demanded, only seconds before the feeling of something—or was it someone—watching her crept over her. Had Caleb found her?

She stiffened as the growl of a wild animal reached her ears. Speed reared up in alarm, dumping her to the ground and galloping off at a faster pace than Danny would have thought possible. She pulled herself up to a sitting position in the dirt.

And froze.

Less than a hundred feet away, a mountain lion was poised, ready to strike. Eyes glistened in the sun, and Daniella, for once in her life, was filled with fear. Her mind wept for the safety of the child inside her. What kind of mother took off for parts unknown, alone, on a questionable horse? She didn't deserve the honor of being a mother.

She sat there, her eyes on the cat that moved forward slowly. She prayed her death would be swift, and God would overlook her failures.

The deep growls of the mountain lion mixed with the palpable sound of her heart. Her fear was tangible. But as she sat there staring back at the animal, the explosive sound of a gunshot joined its scream. But it didn't stop; it kept coming toward her relentlessly.

The hideous sounds in her ears did not stop, either. It took her a moment to realize the screeching noises that remained were coming from her own throat. The echo of a rifle shot pierced the air once more, and the huge cat lay still.

Daniella sat there, unable to breathe. Dazed and shocked at the realization she was still alive, she managed to get to her feet despite shaking from head to foot. She made a circle, trying to see who had fired the weapon that had saved her and saved her child. Her savior was nowhere to be seen, but she caught a flash of sunlight on metal and movement off in the distance, as if someone had just moved from a clearing back into the trees.

Could it be a new threat? Perhaps they were horse-thieves, wanting her mare. Recalling she was also guilty of the latter, could she still be in danger?

Her hand settled on her belly as she tried to plan how to proceed. She was out in the middle of nowhere, right in the center of all the danger and adventure she had come west to find. Caleb would be fit to be tied if he knew the trouble she'd gotten herself into. Here she was, lost in the mountains. No horse. No plan. No sense. No water. Her throat was dry. Her weeping had depleted her.

Was it possible Caleb had been the one who saved her? He might be trailing after her right now, not yet close enough to reach her but close enough to protect her. The solace she took in the thought of him being close by shocked her. Perhaps he *had* been unfaithful, but perhaps he cared enough about her to keep her out of danger, after all. Perhaps…

She shook her head and rubbed the dust off her clothes, forcing herself to begin moving. Feeling sorry for herself was not a choice now. If she was carrying his child, there was only one thing for her to do. It was to keep his baby safe. The time for self-pity would have to wait.

Daniella pondered her choices as she managed to climb the path upward on the long, winding hill ahead. She heaved a sigh of relief as she spotted Speed on the other side, grazing on a patch of thick clover at the bottom of the slope. Thank God, Speed hadn't gone *too* far. There was something to be said for her slowness, after all.

Danny lacked the energy to run after the mare. Instead, she took her time and walked down the slope toward her, singing softly as she approached.

Speed didn't protest as she mounted once again, and she nudged the horse into action. She hoped sincerely they were headed the direction in which Golden River lay.

⁓

Caleb's shoulders sagged with relief as he returned his rifle to the saddle. That was entirely too close. He nudged Socks faster; the distance he'd been following from was too great for comfort. He needed to be closer, in case something else happened. Rattlers were prolific in this territory.

He'd been tracking her for well over two hours, disturbed at the erratic path of Speed's tracks. Did she have the slightest idea how to get to Golden River?

*Damn you, Matthews. All these months, you've accused her of chasing you. Who's doing the chasing now?* His inward lecture made him feel worse as he watched the young woman he loved pick herself up off the ground and walk up the hill to try to find the horse. How far had the animal gotten?

He had a mind to increase his speed, pick her up, and put her on the saddle in front of him. If he did, they'd both get to Golden River in a decent amount of time.

He should have been doing the pursuing from the beginning. Daniella had run from him, and she was putting herself in danger. What made him think he was too good to be a married man, anyway? Tobias seemed to be happy enough. So did Sterling. And his friend, Noah, was miserable because he wanted Jeddah in his arms and in his bed so badly.

Sighing, he stepped up Socks' pace. He was afraid for Daniella to be out of his sight, even for a second.

He suspected she knew she was being followed. An hour and a half later, he was sure of it. When he failed to see her, and Speed's tracks disappeared on the south side of the pass, he knew she'd hidden and waited until he'd gone past her.

*That little brat!* He kept to the path until he had the chance to look back and see her, but when another grove of trees appeared by the path, he brought Socks to a stop inside it.

He didn't have to wait long. Daniella brought Speed by the grove as he waited silently, listening to her sad and weepy little voice pouring out her heart.

He swore to himself if he ever got her home, after he put her over his knee for taking off and stealing the horse from the ladies and putting herself in danger, he'd make her as happy as possible. He wanted to put her in his arms and keep her there.

Deep down, a part of him was extremely proud of his little wife. She'd fought; she'd been unafraid to stand up for herself. But she needed guidance—his guidance—in her life.

And he looked forward to providing it.

# CHAPTER 13

THE DORMITORY...

Daniella had no idea she was being pursued by more than an irate husband. Had she known, she might have increased her pace, but neither she nor the horse seemed in any great rush. Tired and hungry, she realized she had not eaten since breakfast. Glancing up at the sun, it's waning let her know it was late afternoon.

Reaching the top of the next rise, she sighed as Golden River came into view. She was at a loss to understand the strong feelings which overtook her. Home. For the first time in over a month, she felt happy and safe. This was where she belonged. There was a sense of rightness about this place, as if her past and present merged into her future. This was where she was meant to be.

If only she could go back in time. If she'd never left the ranch that fateful morning, how might things be different now? Her rash behavior had caused so much heartache. Perhaps her dreams of ever living a peaceful, happy life as Caleb's wife were gone now. He'd wanted her to wait, but she'd forced his hand.

Well, she couldn't undo the past. What was done was done. Danny decided it was time to start living with the future in mind.

She would give Caleb as much space and time as he wanted. She would not tell anyone about what happened in Sacramento, especially not about them being married. Shaking her head, she realized she might have to confide in Faith and Obie, and at the very least, Jeddah, but she would swear them to silence. No one else need ever know. It would be up to Caleb to decide what happened next.

The dormitory came into view. A weak smile played across Daniella's lips. Less than six months before, this building was a shell, with high hopes of becoming a hotel for the brides of Golden River. The first two such brides had never come to stay there. Now, it was known as a residence for another round of hopeful brides, all seeking to find their happily ever after with a man from the area. She hoped they had better luck than she.

Her stomach began growling loudly as she reached the front of the building. Slowly easing off the horse and making sure to carefully wrap the reins around the post outside, Daniella approached the door and knocked with hesitation. Olivia answered.

She greeted Danny with a surprised expression. "Oh, Daniella, everyone has been wondering where you had gone. Jeddah will be so relieved to see you."

Before she could process Olivia's jumbled words, Danny was ushered inside. "Jeddah is in town today?"

"In town?" Olivia giggled gaily. "She's not only in town, but she's in the kitchen, right now, having coffee. I was just telling her she had to stay for supper. Now, we'll have two guests."

Danny heard a sharp intake of air and turned to see Jeddah emerge from the back of the building. "Danny! You have had us all worried sick!" Within a heartbeat, she found herself pulled tightly to her old friend's chest.

*Home.* Jeddah's sweet fragrance filled her lungs, and Danny fought the tears that threatened. She was safe again. Returning the hug, she felt as if she was no longer facing her problems alone. She was home, surrounded by people who loved her yet knew of all her flaws and still cared enough to worry about her.

A clatter of noise broke her moment of peace. Jeddah walked to the window to see what was causing all the turmoil. "I don't mean to alarm you, Olivia, but the mayor might be bringing in another group of brides. He and Mike Turner are down the road with a wagon load of ladies. Oh, my. If Aunt Faith was here, she would have a fit about what some of the young women are wearing."

Daniella's sense of peace evaporated, and she rushed to have a peek. "Lydia and the girls from the brothel!" It was a whisper, but it was out of her mouth before she even realized it.

"Brothel!" Olivia said, coming to the window to have a look herself. "Mayor Blackaby has gone too far. If he thinks my girls are going to have to contend with such women, he is quite mistaken."

Jeddah and Olivia gawked at the newcomers, but Danny backed away in horror. Her rash deeds from Sacramento had followed her back to Golden River. Pretending nothing had happened the last month was becoming impossible. She longed to pull Jeddah aside and beg for advice, but her emotions reigned at the moment. Danny began to move quietly at first, but as the other girls came forward to see what was happening, she gathered speed and disappeared outside the back door and around the side of the dorm. She had to get to Speed, pull her out of sight, and figure out where to hide.

Daniella came to an abrupt halt as she reached the walkway and rounded the corner. *Speed was gone*.

Spinning around, she searched wildly for the animal, wondering where it could possibly have gone. Muttering to herself, she once again backed between the buildings and began searching for the wayward horse. Her attempt at wrapping the reins around the post must have been poor, after all.

Before she realized how far she had wandered, she gasped. She was less than twenty feet from the sheriff's office. Putting her hand to her lips, she again backed up into the shadows. The last thing she needed was to have Tobias seeing her and calling attention to her.

A curse slipped between her lips when her eyes caught the prancing movement of a horse between the buildings. For a moment, she thought it was Speed.

But, no, it was much worse. Caleb's horse—Socks—was tied outside the building. Desperation took hold, and she started trying to urge the animal to come her way. While her loops were not skilled, Caleb's were spot on. Even when the horse tried to move her way, he was anchored to the post.

Her promises not to act in haste forgotten, she made a desperate decision. The wagon with the ladies from the brothel had reached the center of town and was causing quite a commotion. Seizing her chance, Daniella ran across the street, untied Socks, and mounted.

The ease of which she managed such a bold move made her smile. She was finally beginning to find her way in this Wild West. Why, she doubted any of her friends from back home could have pulled off such a daring move.

It was Caleb's booming voice, however, which pierced the air and caused her heart to sink.

"Daniella, get yourself down from my horse and come over here, right this moment, young lady!"

Without even acknowledging his order, she hunched down over the neck of the horse and urged Socks into a gallop. Heading out of town, she decided there was only one place she could run to now. With any luck, she could hide there until Caleb's temper cooled down. Perhaps by then, Lydia and the ladies would be gone. And hopefully, Jeddah might not realize she had run off again.

~

Caleb watched as his little bride took off on his horse. She was out of sight within seconds. He set his jaw, shaking his head, and set off on foot, deciding to let her get a little ahead.

He knew where she'd be. There was only one place for her to go now. He'd deal with her later for stealing his horse. There was determination in his step, along with the set to his jaw, as he marched after her. He'd seen that look on her face as she'd responded to his command to come to him. Those big brown eyes had been filled with dismay as she turned away to urge Socks out of town. He knew, however, once she reached the ranch, Sterling and Faith would refuse to let her leave. He was sure of that.

So lost in his thoughts, it took moments before he realized the uproar that was happening behind him.

"Follow her!"

He knew that voice; it belonged to Olivia.

"She's stolen Caleb's horse! Look, he's going after her!" Hester's voice, he was sure of it.

"Take us there!" Leanna's voice?

Mike Turner's was next. "If you want to follow them, you can walk, like everyone else."

Overcome by curiosity, Caleb looked backward, over his shoulder. The new brides from the dormitory were hunched up into a bundle, a hundred feet behind.

But another group of ladies followed, a good distance behind and rapidly closing. It was the women from the brothel!

The girls from the dormitory were the closest; he could hear their comments.

"Who are they?"

"I don't know, but they look like trollops."

"Well, they aren't getting *my* man—I'll see to that!"

*Good God. Two gaggles of geese.* The brides were glancing back at them curiously and full of contempt. This very possibly could turn out badly.

Behind them, suddenly, Caleb caught sight of another group. The men of Golden River followed closely. Some looked curious; some looked as if they had a desire to become involved.

Well, he might actually end up needing them, he thought as he heard the approach of galloping horses' hooves. He was amazed. Speed had not moved that fast the entire way back to Golden River. He turned back again, only to see Jeddah on Noah's horse, gaining rapidly.

He heard Noah's voice behind him, shouting for her to stop, but she didn't. She rode as fast as she could toward the ranch, leaving all of them moving like a herd of turtles.

Following the men of town, Noah and Mike Turner hurried their steps. He thought they'd catch up with him any minute.

"Caleb!" It was Noah's voice. "What's going on?"

Caleb ignored the question but shouted back as fast as he could, "Just keep everyone back!"

He could hear Noah's futile attempts to get them to stop. But it was fruitless. No one was listening.

On his last glance back, he caught a glimpse of Mayor Blackaby bringing up the rear, perched precariously atop his donkey. The beast had no desire to move as fast as the mayor demanded. Blackaby was screaming at the animal, and the louder he yelled, the slower it went. Occasionally, it screamed back at him, but it refused to move any faster.

∽

*D*aniella reached the ranch, at last, and exhausted, she slid from Socks. Hearing footsteps, she looked up to see Henry running to her. His face showed his concern.

"Miss Daniella! Are you all right?"

The kindness of his words brought a storm of tears she wasn't even expecting. Leaving him there with a distraught expression, she ran through the front door of the house. The screen door protested as she threw it open, just as it always had.

"Jeddah? Is that you?" Faith's kind voice was heard from the kitchen. Daniella was unable to answer. Instead, she ran up the stairs, trying to keep her sobs as silent as possible. The next thing she heard was a "Well, bless my soul," from Faith, followed by a shout. "Sterling!"

Her old bedroom was just as she had left it. She was grateful for the housekeeper's kindness. She stood there in a haze of tears. It was so good to be home again.

She smiled through her tears. She hadn't thought of any place as being home since she'd left over a month ago. Moving to the window, she dashed the tears away and looked out toward the barn. The sound of thundering horses' hooves caught her attention, and she looked down to see Jeddah, dismounting Noah's gelding.

The next thing she heard was footsteps on the stairs, followed by pounding at her door.

"Danny! Let me in!"

It took seconds for her to reach the door and throw her arms about Jeddah's neck. "Oh, Jeddah! I've ruined everything. *Everything!*"

Jeddah shook her head. "Talk fast, Danny. Caleb will be here any minute. Why is it ruined?"

"Because—I'm carrying his baby!" It came out in a rush, and she watched as Jeddah's beautiful face blanched of color.

Danny stared at her friend for a moment. The room seemed to be swaying. Jeddah was growing further and further away. Putting a shaking hand to her head, she whispered, "I don't feel well," just before crumpling to the floor in a heap.

~

Caleb rushed into the room and stopped abruptly. His little bride was lying in the floor, with Jeddah huddled over her. Both of them were white as sheets.

"Daniella!" Caleb felt his own face growing pale. "Jeddah? What happened? What have you done to her?"

Color began quickly rushing back into Jeddah's cheeks as her eyes grew angry.

He frowned at her reaction. "What did I say? I'm sorry, I didn't mean—"

"Yes, you did." She climbed to her feet, glaring at him. "I swear, Caleb Matthews. How Noah remains your friend is a mystery." She ran to the door, turning back just as she reached it. "It's what you've done to her, you lout. How could you! When I tell Noah, he'll kill you."

"What the devil are you talking about?"

But his question was met with the slam of the door. Jeddah was already gone.

Caleb quickly gathered Daniella into his arms and sat down on the bed, cradling her. He spoke softly into her ear, hoping and praying she would awaken. "Say something, my darling. Please. Tell me you're all right."

"I'm all right." Danny's voice was accompanied by a scowl.

He studied her face blankly. "I'm serious."

She turned her face away. "Doesn't matter. *You* don't care."

Caleb cupped her face and forced her to look up at him. "The hell I don't. What makes you say something like that?"

"You made love to a woman at the brothel."

"Yes, I did. You. A young woman I care for very deeply." He backed up a few inches. "Who did you think I thought I—oh, hell." He shook his head.

"I was dressed up like a virgin bride. That's what you requested, wasn't it?"

"You little idiot. I requested *you*! Madam Lydia sent Leanna to bring you to me. She didn't. Instead, she brought me upstairs to you, all trussed up like a—"

But Danny wasn't listening; that much was obvious.

"Daniella?" His voice was stern this time.

She refused to look at him.

"Are you feeling all right now? And so help me, if you tell me I don't care—"

"I feel quite well, thank you."

"Then answer me this. You can't honestly think I didn't recognize you, can you?" He waited a moment. Daniella turned away again. "All right. You aren't listening, right now. But you will." Immediately, he flipped her over his knee and bared her bottom. A hard hand came down once, twice, a half a dozen times, and she began to try to squirm away from him.

"Stop it, Caleb!"

"I'll stop it when you're ready to listen to me. Not before." He paused, his hand in the air, and began bringing it down once again on her little wiggling bottom. She cried out, but he was determined to keep up the pace until she was willing to be still and listen to what he had to say. He'd waited a long time to say it, and he meant for her to listen.

When he heard a little muffled sob, he stopped. "Ready to hear me now?"

There was a pause, followed by one word, "Yes."

He was unprepared for the meekness in her voice. Turning her in his arms so she faced him, he spoke softly. "All right. Do I have your attention?

She blinked, looking up from his arms, and nodded.

"When we came back to the hotel after we were married and you threw the vase at me—something you'd better *never* do again— and I left you there, I was angry as hell. But do you know who I was angry at?"

Big brown eyes met his. "*Me*," she whispered.

"No. I was angry at myself. Do you understand me?"

"I-I hear you. But I don't understand."

He reached down and moved away a curl that had become wet with tears as he studied her face. "I realized this—our lives, our futures are my responsibility. I knew I loved you. From the very first moment I laid eyes on you, at the ranch, running up the hill with my clothes in your arms—"

"And Noah's."

"And Noah's," he corrected. "But Noah doesn't love you. And he's a more tolerant man than I." He paused. "I hope you realize it, Brat. You're supposed to be listening. Not talking. Understand?"

Another nod.

"As I said, I've loved you a very long time, and I intend—"

She searched his eyes. "Y-you do?"

He silenced for a moment, watching her penitent face. "Listen to me, Daniella. I loved you then, and I love you now. I didn't sleep for days when you left. When I looked all over Sacramento for you, I spoke with a woman at the bar who mentioned the brothel. But I was sure you'd never go there and try to get a job as one of the ladies. When time passed, and I realized it was the only place I hadn't checked, I knew I might have frightened you so badly, you thought there might be no other choice." He held her fast as she tried to move away from him. Again, he pulled her closer, his arms around her tightly.

"I spoke with Madam Lydia. We talked, and I showed her our wedding certificate. And I asked for you. *Only* for you." He brought her closer, almost nose to nose, watching as her eyes grew even wider. "Hear me, Daniella Matthews," he demanded. "I was angry at the girl who took me upstairs, and I was ready to turn around and leave, until I saw you. I knew the moment that adorable little dimple appeared who you were." Leaning down, he kissed her soundly. Staring into her eyes, he gave her a grin. "I love you, my girl. And I want you. *You, and only you*."

The dimple was back, and Caleb leaned down to kiss it.

She reached up a hand to touch his face. "Only me? Um, Caleb? We might, sort of…" She hesitated and sank her teeth into her lower lip. "I mean, we might have a problem."

He stiffened. "What sort of problem?"

"I mean…" She looked away, fighting for words. "I think I'm going to have your baby."

Caleb felt the blood drain from his face as he stared down at her. Then, suddenly, a broad grin made its way across his mouth. Rising to his feet with Daniella still in his arms, he whirled around with her and gave an ear-splitting, howling *whoop* of joy that could be heard all the way downstairs.

# CHAPTER 14

CLASHING...

Outside, Faith and Sterling stood on the front porch, staring in astonishment at the crowd that had formed in their front yard.

Sterling pointed. "This looks bad. I know the men from Golden River. And I recognize the brides."

"So do I. But I don't recognize the group of ladies dressed...so extravagantly. Who do you think they are?"

She need not have asked. Her question was answered quickly, when Olivia turned to face one of the newer ladies, a voluptuous girl with long blonde hair.

"And just who do you think you are?" Olivia's voice carried over everyone else's, enough for Faith and Sterling to hear well. "You look like common trollops."

The young woman had already formed a fist with both hands. Standing straight and tall, she responded quickly, "Think so, do you? You look like common urchins."

Olivia gasped. "How dare you! We're respectable citizens, *unlike* you."

"We've as much right to be here as you. At least, we make our own way. When was the last time *you* worked to make a decent living?"

The situation was deteriorating rapidly.

Faith turned to her husband. "Sterling, do something!"

The wide grin on Sterling's face grew even wider. "I am. I'm watching. And the men are quite enjoying it."

Faith put both hands on her hips as she observed what was taking place. "I can see that. But what I worry about is—" She gasped and put a hand to her mouth. "Oh, dear. Oh, my goodness."

It was a tiny red-haired, green-eyed woman who stepped up and delivered the first punch, right into Olivia's indignant nose. Hester jumped in with the second, and the blonde, well-endowed woman, the third. Suddenly, it seemed as if all of the new brides and every one of the visiting ladies were going at it, tooth and nail. Small fists flew, hatpins appeared, screams were heard, and the sounds of crunching were loud enough to cause pain. Skirts and petticoats were flying, and bare thighs and bottoms were exposed as one girl after another joined in the fray.

The men of Golden River stood back in awe, as if they'd never before witnessed such a scene. Finally, a horse rode up into the yard, and Tobias jumped down. Moving toward the porch, he stared at Sterling. "What the hell's going on? Sterling, why haven't you stopped this?"

Sterling shrugged. "Figured I'd let 'em wear themselves out, first. *You* want to give it a try?"

Tobias glanced from Sterling to the mass of pandemonium in the yard and pulled out his pistol. Holding it up, he fired into the air.

Five seconds went by then ten. Not one single lady paid heed to it. A few seconds later, the sheriff shouted out to the bystanders. "Men!" he called out and moved to grab the nearest young woman by the scruff of the neck and remove her. Setting her down on the ground, he shouted, "Stay. And don't you dare move an inch!"

"Oh, hell." Mike Turner moved in next and took hold of the

beautiful but slightly disheveled redhead. Giving her a hard smack to the bottom, he pulled her out of the crowd and back against him, holding her around the waist. She struggled to get away, but he held her fast. One by one, the men of Golden River followed suit, removing the young women from the fight and threatening them with a trip across the knee if they dared move.

~

Caleb was kissing his bride with all his might, when he heard pounding on the door of Danny's room. He paused, scowling at the door.

"I finally get my wife willingly in my arms and someone has to be banging the door down. "Who the hell is it?" Continuing to hold Daniella with one arm, he moved to the door and jerked it open. Noah stood there in the hallway with Jeddah, looking quite unhappy.

"I still consider you my friend, Caleb. But I want you to know there's a mob down there, demanding you be hung—"

He was interrupted by a shout from Tobias, downstairs, "Get down here, all of you!"

Danny tried to wiggle out of his arms, but Caleb refused to allow her down.

"Caleb! *I can walk*," she protested loudly, but he didn't answer. Carrying her down the stairs, he heard another protest as they reached the bottom.

"Please, Caleb. I want to stand on my own two feet."

He answered with a growl, "All right. But if you start to feel faint—"

"I'll let you know," she finished for him. "I promise."

He stood there a few seconds, unconvinced. At last, he set her on her feet but moved her behind him. "And stay behind me, little one." He took hold of one arm, keeping her there, as he moved out onto the porch. Noah did the same with Jeddah.

Tobias was still trying to calm the crowd as they moved to the front.

"Lynch him!" It was the voice of Hester. Caleb glared at her without speaking.

"Be a responsible man and marry her!" shouted another.

Noah leaned forward and spoke in a low voice. "I'll be glad to perform the ceremony, my friend. But I'm sure you already know that."

"It's a case of loose morals." This time, the voice belonged to a man. "I can tell you that much."

Another voice was heard, and Tobias rolled his eyes. Moving to the edge of the porch, he glared at the crowd. "What's wrong with you? All of you?"

"I can tell you," said a female voice.

Tobias turned to see where the small voice came from, and so did everyone else.

Small but beautiful Madam Lydia pulled away from the arms of Mike Turner and marched forward. Turner made a swipe for her but was too late. She had already reached the porch, and Caleb put a hand down to help her up the steps. A second later, she was standing and staring back at the crowd with her head held high.

"All of you—every single one of you—should grow up." Her voice sounded eloquent but forceful. "You've come to your own self-righteous conclusions and decided you know best, without even thinking there might be an explanation other than your own. What's wrong with you? *I'll* tell you. You're a bunch of small-minded children who have no thought for anyone else's opinions or thoughts. Life isn't always beautiful. Sometimes, it's ugly. Sometimes, it's unpredictable. And sometimes," she added, "it's unjust. Like you."

She stopped speaking and turned toward Caleb. "Show them," she ordered, motioning to his pocket.

Caleb glanced at the crowd. They were quiet now and motionless as they stared at him. Reaching into his pocket, he held up the piece of torn parchment, while Daniella pulled free of his hand. She turned away from the crowd briefly, and when she turned back, in her small hand was the other half. She tried to straighten it as much as possible, and when she held it up to Caleb's, it fit together perfectly.

An *ooh* from Jeddah was echoed by a few others in the crowd.

The redhead turned back to the subdued crowd and spoke again. "Now. If any of you have doubts that Caleb and Daniella are indeed married—and have been for weeks now—you can prove your lack of trust by coming up and taking a look at the dates on their marriage certificate. I, for one, stand with them." Her voice was strong and determined, and she finished by taking a step forward and standing close to Caleb.

Noah brought Jeddah forward and stood on Daniella's other side. "Amen."

At his voice, the other men of Golden River nodded with their own echo of his sentiment, and 'amen' was heard throughout the crowd.

Caleb smiled toward Madam Lydia and drew Daniella into his arms in front of him before the group. Speaking loudly, his voice carried over the property. "I have a confession to make to all of you," he said firmly. "When Daniella and I were first married, and we thought we couldn't make this work, she left me. I didn't know where she was for a long time. It was these lovely ladies who took her in and gave her a safe place to stay, put clothes on her back, and fed her, while I worried myself to death and walked the streets, looking desperately for her. She didn't come back to Golden River then, because she feared you would be too judgmental to accept her back. I pray you'll prove us both wrong. And ladies," he said once again, nodding to Lydia, then Berthie, then Leanna in the crowd, "Daniella and I will always be grateful to you. Thank you."

One by one, people in the yard began to come forward and hug Daniella and Caleb, welcoming them back.

In the midst of the brides, Olivia came to the front. Her nose was quite swollen, and there was a dark bruise under her left eye.

After she hugged Danny and shook Caleb's hand, she turned toward Lydia.

"You were right," she said in a quiet voice. "I was wrong. Please accept my apology and the invitation to stay the night with us at the dormitory? We welcome you."

It was obvious this was hard for her. Caleb and Daniella both watched carefully as Lydia reached out and hugged Olivia back graciously.

"Thank you," Lydia said softly. "I can't tell you how much we appreciate your kindness. I know the ladies will feel the same."

Daniella heaved a sigh in Caleb's arms, and he tightened them around her, leaning down to kiss the top of her head.

Faith stepped forward. "When did you two eat last? Tell me, so I can get the table prepared."

"This little one needs a meal," Caleb answered before Daniella had a chance to speak. "We'd both appreciate your kindness, Faith."

Hearing hoof beats in the yard, everyone there turned to see Mayor Blackaby approach on his donkey. He finally got close enough to dismount and looked around to see that everyone was leaving. It was all over. Dismay settled on his face as he realized he'd missed the whole thing.

"Well, *hell*," he said.

Turner laughed at the look on Blackaby's face. "About time you got here, Mayor. Too lazy to walk, like the rest of us?"

Chuckles broke out among the few remaining men of Golden River. The ranchers, on the other hand, thought it was uproariously funny. It was Faith who shook her head and stared from one to the other. She looked first at Lydia.

"I heard your invitation to go back to the dormitory, but I'll make you another offer. You're welcome to stay here, you and your ladies. Mike Turner, you can stay, as well. Mayor, if it takes as long for you to get home as it did to get here, you'll miss your supper. You can stay, too."

Olivia looked, in truth, relieved and turned to follow the brides back to the dormitory. They were accompanied by several interested men from Golden River and she, ever the concerned mother hen, dared not take her eyes off them. Even Hester was being escorted by one of the men from town.

The crowd had thinned out when Caleb felt a hand on his shoulder. Noah was standing next to him, Jeddah's hand in his. "My apologies. I should have known you'd do the right thing." He put out his hand, and Caleb stared at him for a few seconds before accepting it. When he did, he nodded.

"Thanks, buddy. But you owe me."

Faith's voice caused both of them to turn and stare at her. "All right, Daniella. Follow me to the kitchen. I want to hear it all."

But Caleb held up a hand to stop her. "Daniella is my wife now, Faith. I'll decide if and when—and to whom—she needs to make a confession. And the only person she needs to confess to, right now, is me. I'm sure you'll hear about it, soon enough. But if that isn't enough for you, I'll sick Sterling on you."

Faith stood there, staring blankly at him then at Sterling, who raised a brow at her. A few moments later, she turned and opened the screen door to the house, which gave off its normal annoying protest. She scowled at the door and then tossed her head.

"And would someone please oil the hinges on that damn door!" Letting it close with a slam behind her, she disappeared inside. But she heard Sterling's voice behind her.

"Excuse me," he said with a grin. "I think I need a word with my wife."

~

Supper was delayed but went well. The ranchers came in, clean-shaven and smelling nice, just as they had when the first brides arrived in Golden River. Even Mike and Blackaby had shaved. Danny looked around the table, laughing, until Caleb whispered a warning in her ear.

Tobias had gone back and brought Obedience in, slowly guiding the light carriage, and she looked adorable. Danny ran to hug her as

Tobias brought her into the dining room. But she noticed Jeddah was bouncing in her seat, although she hadn't spoken. Obie was beginning to show, finally, so much more than she had when Danny had left.

It was after the prayer that Noah turned to the rest of the men. "Jeddah and I would like to make an announcement."

The room immediately became silent. Everyone's eyes were on Noah's face.

"A visiting preacher will be here on Sunday morning to bring the sermon."

Grumbles were heard around the room.

"He's the long-winded one."

"We'd rather have you."

"You can't leave us."

Noah put up a hand. "I've no intention of leaving."

Tobias frowned. "Why? Where will you be, then?"

"I," Noah said in his deep voice, "will be spending a few days in private with my bride. Jeddah and I will be married, Saturday morning."

Cheers went up.

"I hope the organist remembers he's supposed to play the *Wedding March*," Jeddah said softly. "He still tries to play *Camptown Races* for hymns every Sunday morning."

Tobias nodded. "He only remembered at our wedding because he was threatened."

Faith was watching Jeddah's face. "Perhaps someone should say something to him."

Sterling grinned. "Well, congratulations, you two. Noah, it's about time for you to learn the famous last words of every married man. Caleb, you, too."

Noah's expression showed surprise. "Words? What words?"

Sterling laughed. He leaned forward, giving Faith a wink and an expression of mirth, and spoke loudly.

"My wife *told* me to."

A siege of laughter filled the room as Sterling gave Faith a hug. But she was not amused.

"I've been telling you to oil the front door for months now and it still squalls every time it's opened," she threw back at him.

"I've been waiting, my dear, to hear you say it one more time."

Faith shook her head, making a face, as Jeddah raised a hand.

"And Danny will stand up with me, now she's home," she announced. "And so will Obie."

Obedience looked worried. "In my condition?"

"You're adorable, just as you are," Tobias said softly. "No one will say a word. If they do, they'll answer to me."

Lydia glanced around the table. "Congratulations, Jeddah. We'd love to stay for it, but I fear we'd best be going back. Everything was left in a state of abandonment."

"It's only two more days," Faith interjected. "You're welcome to stay until then."

"And Blackaby and I could take you all back, Saturday afternoon after the ceremony," Mike offered.

"We would love that," Leanna piped up. Her glance fell to Lydia, and she looked away.

But Lydia only smiled. "Indeed, we would."

Daniella looked up into her husband's face. He looked tired, and she had eaten all she could.

When she caught his eye, he bent down to her ear. "Are you finished, my girl?"

She nodded shyly and smiled. "I think so."

Her husband rose to his feet. "We thank you for the excellent meal, Faith. But I have one tired little bride. I'm taking her upstairs."

Daniella ran to throw her arms around Faith before leaving. Hugging her tightly, she whispered in her ear, "I'll tell you everything, Aunt Faith. Very soon."

The grin that answered was indulgent. "I know," Faith whispered back.

# CHAPTER 15

ABOUT TO BE TAKEN...

Caleb was holding out his hand for her, and she took it. But he didn't allow her to climb the steps on her own. Sweeping her up into his arms, he carried her.

They were halfway up the steps when one of the ranchers came in from the front door, and the hinges screeched.

Daniella cringed at the sound. "Caleb, I order you to go and oil the hinges. Now."

A hard pop was delivered directly to her bottom, and she squealed, "Caleb!"

"In case you missed what I said to Faith earlier, any ordering around here will be done by me. Hear me?"

She sighed, relaxing into his arms. "Yes. But the noise bothers me."

"Does it, now? We'll talk about it. Later."

A moment later, he brought her through the doorway to her room. Standing there, he held her and glanced back toward the door. "Where's the key to the lock?"

Daniella stared up into his face. "I don't know. I never lock it."

A frown creased his forehead. "Never?"

She shook her head. "But no one comes in here without knocking first."

"Not taking a chance."

"On what?"

He carried her over and set her down on the bed, leaning down to touch his forehead to hers. "You are not to move one single inch," he growled, before opening the drawers to the highboy and checking for a key.

"And if I do?"

"Then we'll start our evening with you lying across my knee. You'll be doing that soon enough, anyway." Next, he moved to the vanity, and last, the wardrobe. Finally, he grabbed the chair and angled it under the doorknob, so the door wouldn't open, and turned to grin at her. "Not taking a *chance* on anyone coming in and seeing what I'm about to do to you."

Her eyes widened, and she gulped. "Why, are you going to spank me?"

Undertones of power filled his deep voice when he spoke. "The list is long, you little brat. Running from me the night we married, after I told you to stay there. Putting yourself in danger. Going without meals. Losing weight because of it. Stealing the horse that belonged to the ladies at the brothel. Trying to disguise yourself so I wouldn't recognize you. Hiding, so that I would get ahead of you on the way back to Golden River today. You realize if you'd been behind me when the mountain lion prepared to attack, he'd have gotten you, and I wouldn't have been able to see him to protect you."

"So, it was you—"

"Yes. It was me. And then, stealing Socks after we got back to Golden River." He reached down and lifted her chin. "Shall I go on?"

Daniella felt her eyes grow even larger. "No," she whispered.

"And one more thing, little one. The communication between us absolutely must improve. Do you hear? It *must*. If you feel upset with me to the point you think you must run from me, what will you do in the future?"

She gulped. "Talk to you?"

"Damn right. I demand a promise from you."

She met his eyes and nodded. "I promise. I'll never run away from you again."

"And I promise to do the same if I get upset with you. Those are a few of the things I'll punish you for. But I won't do it today. I finally have you to myself, and I intend to keep you that way. Today, I want to show you how precious you are to me. The punishment will wait." He leaned down to kiss her mouth then her nose. "You, little girl, are about to find out what it's like to be well and truly taken." Tipping her face up to his, he smiled. "The truth is the first night I took you, I was so drunk, I barely remember it. I tried to think about it every day we were apart. And I hated myself for allowing that memory to be stolen by the whiskey. And the second time, I knew who you were. You knew who I was, but we weren't connected. Now is the time, so consider yourself about to be properly and completely ravished."

Her eyes twinkled, her dimple showing in mischievousness. "Oh? And what will you do to me, sir?"

"You'll see." Caleb returned and stood over her. "Keep your eyes on me, And that's an order." Slowly, he began to unbutton his shirt. The trousers came next, and when she lowered her eyes to his member and they widened, he shook his head. "Oh, no. Eyes up here. You don't follow orders well, Daniella. But you'll learn."

Her mouth suddenly dry, she licked her lips, and his eyes narrowed.

"Temptress. Did they teach you that at the brothel?"

Curls shook as she moved her head from side to side. "No, sir. They didn't teach me anything. And they wouldn't allow me upstairs. Madam Lydia insisted on it. Leanna tried to tell me a few things today, before you came in, but I was so upset and scared, I didn't remember any of them."

"Good."

She adopted a sly expression. "Would *you* teach me?"

He stared down at her for a moment, before a slow smile spread across his face. "Will you learn?"

"From you? Of course, sir."

His voice deepened. "See that you do. I expect it."

～

Caleb reached for her waist and put her on her feet beside the bed. He began with her boots, taking one slender ankle in his hands and then the other, removing them. Her stockings were next. He turned her away from him and slowly undressed her, button by button.

She was even smaller with her boots off. His hands glided carefully upward, from her calves, past her knees, and between her thighs. When she gasped, his lopsided smile grew.

He rose to his feet. Carefully, he moved her long curls, so they draped over one shoulder, and began removing her garments, kissing the back of her neck and running his hands through her hair, tugging her head back occasionally to plant another kiss on her temple. He was careful with her gown and placed it over the settee. Running his hands over her waist, he loosened the laces in her corset enough to bring her out of it.

"Such a tiny waist," he growled softly, his voice husky.

Daniella turned to glance over her shoulder uncertainly, and he smiled. The corset gone, he brought his hands toward the front and caressed her breasts softly but firmly, then he smoothed his hands down her waist and to the swell of her bottom. A satisfied groan escaped him as he reached under the garment from behind and brought both hands upward, easing his hands in between her thighs.

Her response was to give a soft moan and close her eyes, and he brought her shift up and removed it, leaving her naked before him.

A hiss escaped her lips, loud enough for him to hear. Turning toward him, she again met his eyes. In the evening light, she instinctively covered her most intimate parts with small hands, until he shook his head.

"No. Hands at your sides and open your eyes." Caleb studied her as she slowly lowered both arms to her sides. Opening her eyes took a little longer. She was a pleasant shade of pink from head to toe, and he gave her an indulgent smile. "You need not be embarrassed, sweetheart. I've seen you before. Remember?"

Nodding, she slowly raised her eyes to his, taking a little time to study his member. But not too long, as if she remembered his orders to keep her eyes on his, she moved them upward quickly.

Gently, he leaned her back against the bed and kissed her soundly, then paused long enough to stare down into her eyes. "Don't be afraid of me." His voice was soft.

Moving down to her right breast, he cupped it gently and sucked at its pebbled tip. The response of it between his lips shot straight to his groin. He brought his hand up gently under the other breast. When Daniella moaned with delight and her eyes closed again, he brought his hand down further, to cup a mound of dark curly hair and push his hand between her silky thighs.

Another moan, and he slid his hands back upward under her arms and brought her to stand. Leaning forward, he brought the pillows from the top of the bed and piled one on top of the other. A husky command escaped. He was losing control, fast.

"Bend over the bed."

Her eyes widened. "Am I doing something wrong?"

He turned her to face the bed, lifting her and placing her face down, until her bottom was high over the pillows and her feet no longer touched the floor.

"No, sweetheart. You're doing everything exactly right. But I want you so badly, I don't think I can wait much longer. You're driving me insane." He separated her thighs carefully from behind, sliding his hands in between them, and began to edge her velvety folds slightly apart.

Daniella's small fists grabbed hold of the coverlet as she gave a soft moan. The urgency in her voice was something he hadn't yet heard from her, and she was thrusting back against his hand. He brought one hand a little forward and began a circling rhythm, and with the other, he entered her channel with one finger. She was tight and clenched down around his finger, her wetness glistening as he brought back his hand. A second finger joined the first as he kept circling. When he removed it, she emitted a bereft little cry.

Caleb smiled, and a moment later, he brought her bottom cheeks slightly apart. This time, he put a well-moistened finger deep into her bottom.

Her head came up off the bed, and her body stiffened with a cry. Immediately she began a frenzied series of movements, accompanied by whimpering cries, lasting a long time. When she finally relaxed into the covers and he saw her hands release their grip, he leaned over her.

"Get used to that, my lovely girl. I'm going to do it a lot in the future."

When a whimper was all that answered, he moved her forward on the bed and climbed up, preparing to repeat his movements. The second time she shattered, he thought she'd never stop. "Daniella," he whispered. "I can't wait any longer. I'm taking you now, but I promise, later, you'll get your turn again. Hear me?"

When she shook her head no, he chuckled. "You liked it, didn't you? Be still now. No. Don't move, babe." Firmly bringing her thighs further apart, he edged closer to her folds and brought the tip inside. "All right?"

Big brown eyes studied him over her shoulder, and she pushed back toward him, impaling herself on him. It nearly was his undoing, and he took hold of her waist firmly.

"I said, be still. Or I won't last five seconds."

Reproachful eyes met his, and he grinned as he thrust in, holding onto her hips. Another thrust, and she closed her eyes in bliss.

"That's my girl. Remain still."

But it seemed impossible for her, and she met his entrance with her bottom thrust toward him. He landed a spank on her right cheek then her left, with a command to stay still, and gripped her hips once more. A series of thrusts followed, gently, at first, but soon becoming merciless.

She cried out just before he gave a guttural groan, and he realized they both had reached their release together.

"Oh, babe," he growled into her ear as he folded her into his embrace, turning her on her side to keep from collapsing on top of her.

"Caleb," her breathy little voice said at last.

"No talking, Daniella. Now's the time to be quiet. Awaken me again in a few moments, and we'll do this again."

A sigh escaped as she snuggled back against him. "That's what I was going to ask." She said triumphantly, "I'd like to, as soon as possible."

Caleb managed to raise up just enough to get a glimpse of her profile. She was leaning her head over on his arm, the smile on her face one of a satisfied woman. The curves of her bottom were nestled close against his groin, and he was unable to believe he was lucky enough to have found someone so precious and so eager to please.

He loved her. He *cherished* her. And he'd never let her go.

# CHAPTER 16

A DELIGHTFUL SURPRISE...

"Wake up, young lady." Caleb's deep voice brought Daniella's eyes open wide. "It's Saturday morning."

She groaned and promptly turned over on her belly. "What time is it?"

"Early. I have a surprise for you."

The beginnings of a scowl changed into expectation. "A surprise? What kind of a surprise? And you didn't answer me."

"The only answer I'll give you is that it's six-thirty. The second one, you'll have to wait for. But knowing you, you'll guess it before we get to the church." He dragged the covers off, leaving her naked, and ran his hand along her spine, pausing long enough to give her bottom a quick pop. "I filled the tub for you, and the water's hot. Take advantage of it while you can, because if you wait too long, it'll get cold. And I'll *still* put you in it."

Daniella wiggled backward and sat up. "You really filled the tub for me?"

He took hold of her waist and set her on the floor. "It's part of your surprise." When she eyed him suspiciously, he chuckled.

"Come with me, brat." Dragging the sheet off the bed, he wrapped it around her and lifted her into his arms, carrying her out into the hallway and toward the bath.

Daniella tilted her head. "Come with me? I don't seem to have much choice, do I?" A giggle escaped. He was closing the door to the bath behind them and turning the key in the lock.

"Nope. Stop complaining. You didn't have to lift a finger."

She sighed blissfully as he lowered her down into the hot water. "Oh, this is heavenly, Caleb, thank you. I suppose I'd better not stay too long. Aunt Faith will need help downstairs with breakfast."

"Madam Lydia is down there helping. So is Leanna. And Berthie is trying to tell Faith how to cook breakfast."

"Oh, dear."

"Yes. And *you* are not to be doing anything, today."

She blinked up at him. "I suppose we'll have to stop calling her madam, since she and Mike are getting married."

"I suppose. And it looks like Leanna and Blackaby are, too. She's already talked him into buying a horse and carriage and giving the donkey to Noah for the farm."

"*Giving* the donkey to Noah? The mayor? Are you sure we're discussing the same man?"

"I hear you, brat. Can you believe it? My own opinion is he and Leanna are well suited for one another." Danny's musical laugh brought a grin to Caleb's face. "He's downstairs, as well. And Faith is at the end of her patience. She can't abide him, in case you hadn't noticed. Here, tilt your head back."

Daniella glanced upward. "Why?"

"Because I'm going to wash your hair, that's why."

"Caleb?" There was awe in Daniella's voice. "This is turning out to be a very nice surprise."

He gave her a lopsided grin. "You haven't seen it all yet. Close your eyes, so I don't get soap in them."

There was a pause while she obeyed, and the pleasant scent of castile met her nose. Gentle hands began lathering up the soap into her hair, and she gave a contented sigh. "Caleb?"

"Yes, sweetheart?"

"Have I told you how much I love you?"

He laughed. "No. But I knew it. Always."

"Well, I do. I love you with all my heart."

"Good. Be still while I rinse your hair."

If she was expecting a declaration in return, she was disappointed. Daniella remained still as he rinsed with the rosemary tea, and she felt a kiss on her forehead.

"I hate to leave you, but I have something I need to do. I'll be back to get you in a few moments. Don't leave the bath until then. Hear me?"

"Yes, sir," she said uncertainly.

"I mean it."

She watched him as he rose to his feet and turned back to give her a wink before leaving the room, wondering what he was up to this morning.

The last two days had been wonderful. He'd taken her to bed so many times, she'd lost count. He'd awakened her in the middle of the night and loved her, he'd taken her on the settee, on the floor. Once he'd taken her for a walk in the woods and took her on her belly, lying over a log. He'd positioned her in ways she'd never even thought possible. And she had loved every minute of it.

She was still lying back in the tub when she heard his voice, above her in the room. "Ready? Ah, have you gone to sleep?"

Daniella opened her eyes to find his handsome face above hers. "No. I was thinking."

"About me, I hope."

A blush settled across her cheeks. "Yes."

His answering half-smile brought a twinkle to her eyes. Reaching into the water, he scooped her up and stood her on her feet. After scrubbing her dry with the towel, he again wrapped the sheet around her and carried her to the bedroom. But he stopped as soon as he reached the door.

"Close your eyes."

"What?"

"You heard me. Close them."

Daniella obeyed but slowly. Finally, he moved with her, and she heard the door close once again.

"Keep them closed."

"What are you doing?"

"You'll see." She was set down on her feet suddenly. "Wait here. And don't move."

The sound of a chair as it was dragged over reached her ears, and she felt something brush the back of her legs.

"Now, open your eyes."

She opened, first one, squinting at him, and then the other.

And then, she saw it. On the bed, lay the gown she'd made to get married in. Next to it were dainty satin slippers.

Daniella stood there, unable to breathe. When air finally did pass her lungs, she looked up with tears filling her eyes. "Caleb?"

His smile was indulgent, his own eyes twinkling. Pressing her down into the chair, he took both her hands in his.

"You're shaking. Listen to me, little one. You've been robbed of the wedding you dreamed of. You've even been denied the proposal you deserved. So, here it is."

She gulped, watching as he got down on one knee and brought one hand, then the other, to his lips and kissed them. "My beautiful little Daniella, I would be honored and delighted if you would agree to be my wife for the rest of our days."

"B-but..." she stammered. "I'm already your wife."

"Yes. By law you are. But I'm asking you, because I want you to know you're not only loved but desired, cherished, and adored. I wish, sweetheart, for you to be by my side now and in an hour, a week...a year. I want you the rest of my life. Forever. Do you understand?"

Sobs burst forth from her at the words she'd never thought she'd hear, and Caleb took her in his arms. "Are you t-truly s-serious?"

"Never more serious than right now. I want to dress you in the gown you made, and Noah and Jeddah have agreed to allow us to renew those vows we made over a month ago, along with them, this morning. I sent Henry to Sacramento the day before yesterday to retrieve your trunks, so you could wear your gown."

Her sobs grew louder, and Caleb's face became alarmed. "Daniella? What is it? Are you refusing me?"

"No! How could I? Oh, Caleb, how can you know what this means to me?"

"Oh, Lord. You're happy? But you're *weeping?* How am I supposed to understand this?" He held her back from him. "Do all females do this?"

"I'm happier than I've ever been. In my whole life." She reached toward him, and he pulled her close, holding her tightly. "We're going to have to come to some agreement here, little one. If you're happy but you're sobbing, you'll have to tell me what you're really feeling. Promise me."

She was sniffling now. "I promise."

"But you didn't answer me. Will you marry me again, today?"

She snuggled into his neck. "Oh, Caleb. *Yes*."

She felt him give a relieved sigh and nestled even closer into his neck. And she knew when he raised her chin to kiss her, he wanted her for his wife as much as she wanted him for her husband.

∽

Two hours later, Caleb and Noah stood in front of the visiting minister, listening to him as he gathered the information on each couple. He questioned Noah first, satisfied with his answers, and then turned to Caleb for the third time.

"I'm confused, Mr. Matthews. The young lady's last name is Matthews, as well?"

"Yes."

"Who is she?"

Caleb had already been through this twice. "Daniella Matthews is my wife. We want to review our vows in front of the citizens of Golden River."

"Review."

"Yes."

"Not renew."

"Review or renew, it doesn't matter. We were married in Sacramento, away from our home, and she didn't get to wear her wedding dress, and she was away from home, and we—oh, hell."

"Excuse me, young man!"

"He's frustrated, sir," interjected Noah.

"I don't need you to take up for me, buddy," Caleb threw back.

"Who married you?" the minister interrupted. Both men turned to look at him.

"Father McKnight."

The minister looked confused. "You're Catholic?"

"No."

"She's Catholic, then."

"No. Look, neither of us is Catholic. But we had to agree to raise our children Catholic, and we don't wish to do that—"

"Ah, I see. Why didn't you just say so?"

The look on Caleb's face was one of complete confusion as he blinked and raised one eyebrow. Turning to Noah, he was met with a grin.

"Noah?"

"Yes, my friend."

"Not a word."

The minister looked at his notes again. "All right. I believe we're ready." He paused as music in the main auditorium began to play. "There's an organist here? I do say, it sounds strangely like—"

"I know, I *know*," Caleb muttered under his breath. "*Camptown Races*. Excuse me, sir."

Caleb closed the door behind him and nodded to the auditorium full of people of Golden River. He tipped his hat to them and wandered quietly over to the organist, who was attempting to keep the pedals going. It had the distinct sound of a calliope, and Caleb, reaching down, brought the gentleman straight up out of his chair.

"Do you remember a few months ago, sir, when you played for the wedding of Tobias Madison and Obedience Bartlett?"

The organist's eyes grew wider, and he nodded. "They were quite insistent about—"

"Yes, and so am I. Look toward the back of the church, sir. Do you see that lovely little dark-haired girl?"

"I do, yes."

Caleb forced a smile. "That young lady was denied a proper wedding a few weeks ago, and I have promised her one. She will not come down the aisle to the tune of *Camptown Races*. She will come down to the *Wedding March* and nothing else."

"I see."

"And I know from the sheriff's wedding, you are fully capable of playing the *Wedding March*. And," he leaned forward, "if I so much as hear one single *do dah*, I will personally come over, and this will become a funeral instead of a wedding. Do you understand?"

The growl in Caleb's voice brought the man's eyes open further. He took a deep breath.

"I understand, sir."

"Very good." Caleb dusted off the front of organist's shirt. "Then, you may begin." He continued to stand there until the organist sat down and pumped the pedals a few times. The *Wedding March* began to wheeze out of the instrument, and Caleb nodded and moved back to the office. Opening the door, he motioned the minister out front, followed by Noah, who seemed to be hiding laughter behind a cough.

Obedience came down the aisle first, escorted by Tobias. She was showing just enough to make her look adorable, and there were *oohs* and *ahhs* from the church where the newest brides sat. Then Sterling came forward, with Jeddah on one arm and Daniella on the other. He glanced at Noah, who had eyes only for Jeddah, and watched as Danny moved forward.

She was breathtaking. Never had he seen a more enchanting creature. He waited until his bride was all the way down front, before moving to stand next to her and putting his arm around her waist.

She returned his grin with a beautiful smile. Both dimples were showing, this time. The music had stopped, and the minister had begun speaking, droning on in his monotone voice.

Caleb didn't care. He heard very little of what the minister said. He had eyes only for Daniella, with her big brown eyes glancing up in his direction periodically.

The minister managed to pair the names wrong, not once, but twice. It didn't matter. If Daniella hadn't giggled, he might have missed it completely.

But he found himself holding his breath when it was time for Daniella to say the final *I do* and then relaxed. As the minister made the introductions, Noah turned to kiss Jeddah briefly in front of the crowd. Caleb, however, reached for Daniella and lifted her off her feet, taking his fill of her mouth before setting her back down on her little slippered feet.

"I feel as if you're mine, at last," he breathed into her ear as he guided her out the front door of the church.

Daniella stopped and faced him, putting a small hand to his cheek.

"Oh, Caleb," she whispered softly. "*I've always been yours.*"

# EPILOGUE

FAMOUS LAST WORDS...

*T*he wedding reception that Faith held at the ranch was attended by everyone in Golden River. But the little town seemed more unsettled than ever, in some respects. Mike Turner and Mayor Blackaby were getting the wagon ready to take the ladies back to Sacramento, but it was to be a brief trip. The original trip, planned only to drop the ladies off, turned out to be a trip to pick up their belongings and bring them back to the ranch until they were married. In the two days prior to Daniella and Caleb's arrival back, every single one of the ladies from the brothel had gotten engaged. Even Berthie had decided to make Golden River her new home, and she planned to open a little restaurant in town.

Many of the brides in town had also decided to marry. *Funny thing*, Caleb decided as he watched the brides enter for the reception on the arms of the very men who had pulled them from the fight two days before.

He observed his own little bride as she ate a small amount, and her eyes began to show heavy lids. He'd noticed that about her the past few days. Making his way over to her, he leaned down into her ear. "You're tired, sweetheart."

She looked up. "A little."

"I'm taking you upstairs for a nap. Don't argue."

"Can I sleep in your arms?"

"Do you promise to sleep?"

When she hesitated, he lifted her off her feet. "All right. I'll see to it you do."

Allowing her to say a goodbye to the crowd, he carried her upstairs. But when the front door springs were heard in response to the door being opened, Daniella rolled her eyes heavenward and put her head down on his shoulder. But she remained silent.

Caleb brought her to the bed and out of her gown before leaning down and kissing her mouth. "I'll be right back," he promised.

A pout formed on her mouth, and he ran his fingers gently over her lips. "Shhh," was all he said before leaving the room.

~

*H*e was down on his knees by the door, with the oil can in his hand, when he heard a voice from above him. "What are you doing down there?" It was Mike's booming voice he heard.

Caleb glanced up with a frown to see Turner and Lydia, their arms linked. "Quiet," Caleb ground out. "I swear, Turner, they can hear you in Sacramento."

Mike dropped to his knees. "Sorry. What are you doing down here?"

"What does it look like? I'm oiling the hinges before I go back upstairs to Daniella."

They both stared at each other, and Caleb grinned, first at Lydia and then at Turner. One final sentence escaped as he returned to what he was doing, "My wife *told* me to."

# The End

# PIPPA GREATHOUSE

Pippa Greathouse has been writing since the fifth grade, after each student was given an assignment to read aloud a story to the class of their writing. One horrified teacher later, and a class of students who thought the horror story was "cool," and she was hooked.

She is married, and has two fantastic children, who have grown and left the nest.

Since then, the writing has continued. She now is an author for Blushing Books, and still loves what she does. Her favorite genre is writing historical fiction romances, where men are "strong, Alpha men" and their feisty ladies respond to that. And historical fiction is perfect for that! However, she also loves writing contemporary romantic fiction.

*Don't miss these exciting titles by Pippa Greathouse and Blushing Books!*

Time for Change
Macie's War
Catching Carrie

*Pike's Bluff Series*
Double-Takes
Night-Silences

*The Conquered Series (With Ruby Caine)*
Conquered by the Captain, Book One
Conquered by the Commander, Book Two
Conquered by the Ghost, Book Three

*The Unsettling of Golden River (With Ruby Caine)*
Being Obedient, Book One
Daring Daniella, Book Two

*The Strasburg Chronicles*
Angelica's Rescuer: Book One
Merrie's Hero: Book Two
Cinderella's Lawman: Book Three
The Return Of Lucy Grace: Book Four
Miriam's Rebirth: Book Five

*Strasburg: The New Generation*
Judging Cicely, Book One
Katie's Maverick, Book Two

*Audiobooks*
Angelica's Rescuer

pippagreathouse.com

# RUBY CAINE

Ruby Caine is an exclusive Blushing author. She lives near New Orleans, Louisiana, and the region is the setting for most of her works. Caine writes contemporary romances and co-authors historical novels with Pippa Greathouse. Married for almost 30 years, she and her beloved husband have four children, two grandchildren and way too many pets. (That last notion comes from her mate, who frowns on taking in stray animals but can't quite stop his wife from doing so.)

Don't miss these exciting books by Ruby Caine and Blushing Books!

*The Spirits of River Oaks*
Her Man, His Rules
(Includes: Her Chance Encounters,
The Royal Psychic,
Haunting Memories and
Running from her Fate)

*Louisiana Loving*
Meeting Jean Deaux, Book One
Meeting Paul Deaux, Book Two
Meet the Deaux Brothers (Books One and Two)
Meeting Eve Deaux

*Katrina's Aftermath series*
Real Reality, Book One
Talk Dirty to Me, Book Two

Cajun Charmer, Book Three
Taming His Creole Beauty, Book Four
Katrina's Aftermath, 4-book set

The Unsettling of Golden River (With Pippa Greathouse)
Being Obedient, Book One
Daring Daniella, Book Two

*The Conquered Series (With Pippa Greathouse)*
Conquered by the Captain, Book One
Conquered by the Commander, Book Two
Conquered by the Ghost, Book Three

*Single Titles*
Making the Wright Connections

*Connect with Ruby Caine:*
*rubycaine.com*

Milton Keynes UK
Ingram Content Group UK Ltd.
UKHW040135170224
437973UK00001B/22